Translated Language Learning

Alice's Adventures in Wonderland

مغامرات أليس في بلاد العجائب

Lewis Carroll

لويس كارول

English / العربية

Down the Rabbit Hole
أسفل حفرة الأرانب

Alice was beginning to get very tired

بدأت أليس تتعب جدا

she was sitting by her sister on the grass bank

كانت تجلس بجانب أختها على الضفة العشبية

but she had nothing to do

لكن لم يكن لديها ما تفعله

her sister was reading a book

كانت أختها تقرأ كتابا

once or twice Alice peeped into the book

مرة أو مرتين نظرت أليس إلى الكتاب

but the book had no pictures or conversations in it

لكن الكتاب لم يكن يحتوي على صور أو محادثات

"what use is a book without pictures?," thought Alice

"ما فائدة الكتاب بدون صور؟" ، فكرت أليس

"why would a book have no conversations?"

"لماذا لا يحتوي الكتاب على محادثات؟"

but she had other things to consider

لكن كان لديها أشياء أخرى يجب مراعاتها

"making a chain of daisies would be a pleasure"

"سيكون من دواعي سروري صنع سلسلة من الإقحوانات"

"but is it worth the effort of getting up and picking the daisies??"

"لكن هل يستحق الأمر الجهد المبذول للنهوض والتقاط الإقحوانات ؟؟"

this was not so easy to think about

لم يكن من السهل التفكير في هذا

because the day was making her feel sleepy and stupid

لأن اليوم كان يجعلها تشعر بالنعاس والغباء

but suddenly her thoughts were interrupted

لكن فجأة انقطعت أفكارها

a White Rabbit with pink eyes ran close by her

ركض أرنب أبيض بعيون وردية بالقرب منها

There was nothing overly remarkable about the rabbit

لم يكن هناك شيء رائع للغاية حول الأرنب

and Alice did not think the rabbit remarkable either

ولم تعتقد أليس أن الأرنب رائع أيضا

nor did it surprise her when the Rabbit spoke

ولم يفاجئها عندما تحدث الأرنب

"Oh dear! I shall be too late!" he said to himself

"يا عزيزي! سأكون متأخرا جدا!" قال لنفسه

but then the Rabbit did something that rabbits didn't do

ولكن بعد ذلك فعل الأرنب شيئا لم تفعله الأرانب

the Rabbit took a watch out of its waistcoat-pocket

أخرج الأرنب ساعة من جيب صدرية

he looked at the time and then hurried on

نظر إلى الوقت ثم سارع

Alice got to her feet, in amazement

وقفت أليس على قدميها في دهشة

she had never seen a rabbit with a waistcoat before!

لم تر أرنبا بصدرية من قبل!

nor had she ever seen a rabbit with a watch!

ولم تر أرنبا يحمل ساعة!

Alice was burning with a new curiosity

كانت أليس تحترق بفضول جديد

and she ran across the field after the Rabbit

وركضت عبر الحقل بعد الأرنب

she was just in time to see the rabbit disappear

كانت في الوقت المناسب لرؤية الأرنب يختفي

the rabbit hopped down into a large rabbit-hole

قفز الأرنب إلى حفرة أرنب كبيرة

In another moment, down went Alice after the rabbit!

في لحظة أخرى ، ذهبت أليس بعد الأرنب!

The rabbit-hole went straight on like a tunnel

سارت حفرة الأرانب مباشرة مثل النفق

and the tunnel kept going for some distance

واستمر النفق في السير لبعض المسافة

and then the path suddenly dipped down

ثم انخفض المسار فجأة

Alice had not a moment to think about stopping herself

لم يكن لدى أليس لحظة للتفكير في إيقاف نفسها

she found herself falling down and down and down

وجدت نفسها تسقط وتسقط وهبوطا

it seemed as if she had fallen down a very deep well

بدا الأمر كما لو أنها سقطت في بئر عميق جدا

Either the well was very deep, or she fell very slowly

إما أن البئر كانت عميقة جدا ، أو سقطت ببطء شديد

because she had plenty of time to fall

لأن لديها متسعا من الوقت لتسقط

as she was falling she could look all around her

بينما كانت تسقط ، كان بإمكانها أن تنظر حولها

First, she tried to make out where she was going

أولا ، حاولت معرفة إلى أين هي ذاهبة

but the well was too dark to see anything

لكن البئر كان مظلما جدا بحيث لا يمكن رؤية أي شيء

then she looked at the sides of the well

ثم نظرت إلى جوانب البئر

and she noticed that there were cupboards all around her

ولاحظت أن هناك خزائن في كل مكان حولها

and all around the well were book-shelves

وفي كل مكان حول البئر كانت أرفف الكتب

here and there she saw maps and pictures hung upon pegs

هنا وهناك رأت خرائط وصورا معلقة على أوتاد

She took down a jar from one of the shelves as she passed

أنزلت جرة من أحد الرفوف أثناء مرورها

the jar was labelled for its content

تم تصنيف الجرة لمحتواها

"MARMALADE MADE FROM ORANGES"

"مربى البرتقال مصنوع من البرتقال"

but, to her great disappointment, the marmalade jar was empty

ولكن ، لخيبة أملها الكبيرة ، كانت جرة مربى البرتقال فارغة

she did not want to drop the empty marmalade jar

لم تكن تريد إسقاط جرة مربى البرتقال الفارغة

and her fall was very slow

وكان سقوطها بطيئا جدا

so she managed to put the marmalade jar into one of the cupboards

لذلك تمكنت من وضع جرة مربى البرتقال في إحدى الخزائن

Down, down, down she fall!

لأسفل ، لأسفل ، لأسفل تسقط!

Would the fall ever come to an end?

هل سينتهي السقوط؟

There was nothing else to do

لم يكن هناك شيء آخر تفعله

so Alice soon began talking to herself

لذلك سرعان ما بدأت أليس في التحدث إلى نفسها

"Dinah will miss me very much tonight, I should think!"

"دينا ستفتقدني كثيرا الليلة ، يجب أن أعتقد!"

Dinah was Alice's cat

كانت دينا قطة أليس

"I hope they'll remember her saucer of milk at tea-time"

"آمل أن يتذكروا صحن الحليب الخاص بها في وقت الشاي"

"Dinah, my dear, I wish you were down here with me!"

"دينا ، عزيزتي ، أتمنى لو كنت هنا معي!"

Alice felt that she was dozing off

شعرت أليس أنها كانت تغفو

and then suddenly, thump! thump!

ثم فجأة ، ضرب! رطم!

down she fell upon a heap of sticks

سقطت على كومة من العصي

and she landed on a pile of dry leaves

وهبطت على كومة من الأوراق الجافة

and finally the long fall down the hole was over

وأخيرا انتهى السقوط الطويل في الحفرة

Alice was not a bit hurt

لم تتأذى أليس قليلا

and she jumped up within a moment

وقفزت في غضون لحظة

She looked up, but it was all dark overhead

نظرت إلى الأعلى ، لكن كل شيء كان مظلما في السماء

in front of her was another long corridor

أمامها كان هناك ممر طويل آخر

and the White Rabbit was still in sight

وكان الأرنب الأبيض لا يزال في الأفق

he was hurrying down the corridor

كان يسرع في الممر

There was not a moment to be lost

لم تكن هناك لحظة نضيعها

off ran Alice like the wind

ركض أليس مثل الريح

around the corner turned the rabbit

قاب قوسين أو أدنى تحول الأرنب

she was just in time to hear the rabbit

كانت في الوقت المناسب لسماع الأرنب

""Oh, my ears and whiskers"

""أوه ، أذني وشعيراتي"

"how late it's getting!"

"كم تأخر الوقت!"

She was close behind the rabbit

كانت قريبة من الأرنب

she turned around another corner

استدارت حول زاوية أخرى

but the Rabbit was no longer to be seen

لكن الأرنب لم يعد يمكن رؤيته

She found herself in a long, low hall

وجدت نفسها في قاعة طويلة منخفضة

the hall was lit up by a row of ceiling lamps

أضاءت القاعة بصف من مصابيح السقف

There were doors all around the hall

كانت هناك أبواب في جميع أنحاء القاعة

but all the doors were locked

لكن جميع الأبواب كانت مغلقة

she walked all the way down one side of the hall

سارت على طول الطريق على جانب واحد من القاعة

and she had walked all the way up the other side of the hall

وقد سارت على طول الطريق على الجانب الآخر من القاعة

she had tried every door

لقد جربت كل باب

and she walked sadly down the middle of the hall

وسارت بحزن في منتصف القاعة

"how am I ever going to get out again?"

"كيف سأخرج مرة أخرى؟"

Suddenly she came upon a little table

فجأة جاءت على طاولة صغيرة

the table was made entirely of solid glass

كانت الطاولة مصنوعة بالكامل من الزجاج الصلب

There was nothing on the table but a tiny golden key

لم يكن هناك شيء على الطاولة سوى مفتاح ذهبي صغير

the key might belong to one of the doors!

قد ينتمي المفتاح إلى أحد الأبواب!

but, alas! some of the locks were too large for the keys

لكن ، للأسف! كانت بعض الأقفال كبيرة جدا بالنسبة للمفاتيح

and for the other locks the key was too small

وبالنسبة للأقفال الأخرى ، كان المفتاح صغيرا جدا

but, at any rate, the key opened none of the doors

ولكن ، على أي حال ، لم يفتح المفتاح أيا من الأبواب

but what was she to do?

لكن ماذا كانت تفعل؟

she went through the hall again

ذهبت عبر القاعة مرة أخرى

and this time she noticed a low curtain

وهذه المرة لاحظت ستارة منخفضة

behind the curtain was a little door

خلف الستارة كان هناك باب صغير

the door was about fifteen inches high

كان ارتفاع الباب حوالي خمسة عشر بوصة

She tried the little golden key in the lock

جربت المفتاح الذهبي الصغير في القفل

and to her great delight, the key fit in the lock!

ومما يسعدها أن المفتاح يناسب القفل!

Alice opened the door

فتحت أليس الباب

and she found the door led into a small corridor

ووجدت الباب يؤدي إلى ممر صغير

the corridor was not much larger than a rat-hole

لم يكن الممر أكبر بكثير من حفرة الفئران

she knelt down and looked along the corridor

ركعت على ركبتيها ونظرت على طول الممر

and she saw the loveliest garden you have ever seen

ورأت أجمل حديقة رأيتها على الإطلاق

how she longed to get out of that dark hall

كيف كانت تتوق للخروج من تلك القاعة المظلمة

how she wanted to wander among those bright flowers

كيف أرادت أن تتجول بين تلك الزهور الزاهية

how cool refreshing those fountains looked

كم بدت تلك النوافير المنعشة الرائعة

but she could not even get her head through the doorway

لكنها لم تستطع حتى إدخال رأسها عبر المدخل

"Oh," said Alice, mournfully

"أوه" ، قالت أليس بحزن

"how I wish I could fold up like a telescope!"

"كم أتمنى أن أتمكن من طي مثل التلسكوب!"

"I think I could fold up like a telescope"

"أعتقد أنني أستطيع الطي مثل التلسكوب"

"if I only knew how to begin"

"لو كنت أعرف فقط كيف أبدأ"

Alice went back to the table

عادت أليس إلى الطاولة

there was the chance of finding another key

كانت هناك فرصة للعثور على مفتاح آخر

or there might be a book of rules

أو قد يكون هناك كتاب من القواعد

the book could tell her how to fold up like a telescope

يمكن أن يخبرها الكتاب كيف تطوى مثل التلسكوب

This time she found a little bottle

هذه المرة وجدت زجاجة صغيرة

"this bottle certainly was not here before," said Alice

قالت أليس: "هذه الزجاجة بالتأكيد لم تكن هنا من قبل"

and tied around the neck of the bottle was a paper label

وكان مربوطا حول عنق الزجاجة ملصق ورقي

the label was beautifully printed in large letters

تمت طباعة الملصق بشكل جميل بأحرف كبيرة

"DRINK ME"

"اشربني"

"No, I'll look first," she said

قالت: "لا ، سأنظر أولا"

"I'll see whether the bottle is marked as poisonous or not,"

"سأرى ما إذا كانت الزجاجة تحمل علامة سامة أم لا ،"

because she never forgot the lesson about poison

لأنها لم تنس أبدا درس السم

"if a bottle is labelled poisonous, it's bound to disagree with you"

"إذا تم تصنيف الزجاجة على أنها سامة ، فلا بد أن تختلف معك"

However, this bottle was not marked as poisonous

ومع ذلك ، لم يتم تمييز هذه الزجاجة على أنها سامة

so Alice ventured to taste the content of the bottle

لذلك غامرت أليس بتذوق محتوى الزجاجة

she found the liquid quite to her liking

لقد وجدت السائل يرضيها تماما

the drink had a sort of mixed flavour

كان للمشروب نوع من النكهة المختلطة

cherry-tart, custard, and pineapple

تارت الكرز والكاسترد والأناناس

roast turkey, toffee, and toast with hot butter

الديك الرومي المشوي والتوفي والخبز المحمص بالزبدة الساخنة

and she soon finished off the bottle

وسرعان ما أنهت الزجاجة

"What a curious feeling!" said Alice

"يا له من شعور غريب!" قالت أليس

"I am folding up like a telescope!"

"أنا مطوي مثل التلسكوب!"

And she was folding up like a telescope indeed!

وكانت تطوي مثل التلسكوب بالفعل!

She was now only ten inches high

كان ارتفاعها الآن عشر بوصات فقط

and her face brightened up at her thoughts

وأشرق وجهها من أفكارها

now she was the the right size for the little door

الآن كانت بالحجم المناسب للباب الصغير

now she could go into that lovely garden

الآن يمكنها الذهاب إلى تلك الحديقة الجميلة

soon she stopped getting smaller

سرعان ما توقفت عن الصغر

she decided on going into the garden at once

قررت الذهاب إلى الحديقة على الفور

but, alas for poor Alice!

لكن ، للأسف لأليس المسكينة!

she got to the door

وصلت إلى الباب

but she had forgotten the little golden key

لكنها نسيت المفتاح الذهبي الصغير

she went back to the table for the key

عادت إلى الطاولة للحصول على المفتاح

but she found she could not reach high enough

لكنها وجدت أنها لا تستطيع الوصول إلى عال بما فيه الكفاية

she could see the key quite plainly through the glass

كان بإمكانها رؤية المفتاح بوضوح تام من خلال الزجاج

she tried to climb up the legs of the table

حاولت تسلق أرجل الطاولة

but the glass was far too slippery

لكن الزجاج كان زلقا جدا

eventually she tired herself out with trying

في النهاية تعبت نفسها من المحاولة

and the poor little girl sat down and cried

وجلست الفتاة الصغيرة المسكينة وبكت

Alice spoke to herself rather sharply

تحدثت أليس إلى نفسها بحدة إلى حد ما

"Come, there's no use in crying like that!"

"تعال ، لا فائدة من البكاء بهذه الطريقة!"

"I advise you to stop right this minute!"

"أنصحك بالتوقف في هذه اللحظة!"

She generally gave herself very good advice

لقد أعطت نفسها بشكل عام نصيحة جيدة جدا

though she very seldom followed her own advice

على الرغم من أنها نادرا ما اتبعت نصيحتها الخاصة

and she sometimes was too harsh on herself

وكانت في بعض الأحيان قاسية جدا على نفسها

and her words brought tears into her eyes

وجلبت كلماتها الدموع في عينيها

Soon her eye fell upon a little glass box

سرعان ما سقطت عينها على صندوق زجاجي صغير

the little glass box was lying under the table

كان الصندوق الزجاجي الصغير ملقى تحت الطاولة

in the glass box was a very small cake

في الصندوق الزجاجي كانت كعكة صغيرة جدا

on the cake some words were beautifully written

على الكعكة كانت بعض الكلمات مكتوبة بشكل جميل

the words had been marked in currants

تم تمييز الكلمات بالكشمش

"EAT ME"

"تناولني"

"Well, I'll eat the cake," said Alice

قالت أليس "حسنا ، سآكل الكعكة"

"and if the cake makes me grow larger, I can reach the key"

"وإذا كانت الكعكة تجعلني أكبر ، يمكنني الوصول إلى المفتاح"

"and if the cake makes me grow smaller, I can creep under

the door"

"وإذا جعلتني الكعكة أصغر, يمكنني أن أتسلل تحت الباب"

"so either way I'll get into the garden"

"لذا في كلتا الحالتين سأدخل الحديقة"

"and I don't care which of the two happens!"

"ولا يهمني أي من الاثنين يحدث!"

She ate a little bit of the cake

أكلت القليل من الكعكة

and she anxiously spoke to herself:

وتحدثت بقلق إلى نفسها:

"Which way? Which way?"

"في أي اتجاه؟ في أي اتجاه؟"

and she held her hand on her head

وأمسكت يدها على رأسها

she wanted to feel which way she was growing

أرادت أن تشعر بالطريقة التي كانت تنمو بها

she was quite surprised to find what had happened

لقد فوجئت تماما بالعثور على ما حدث

she had remained the same size!

لقد بقيت بنفس الحجم!

so this time she doubled her efforts

لذلك ضاعفت هذه المرة جهودها

and soon she finished off the whole cake

وسرعان ما أنهت الكعكة بأكملها

The Pool of Tears
بركة الدموع

"This is getting more and more interesting!" cried Alice

"هذا يزداد إثارة للاهتمام!" صرخت أليس

You can see she was very surprised

يمكنك أن ترى أنها كانت مندهشة جدا

"I'm opening out like the largest telescope there ever was!"

"أنا أفتح مثل أكبر تلسكوب على الإطلاق!"

"Good-bye, feet! Oh, my poor little feet"

"وداعا أيها القدمين! أوه ، قدمي الصغيرة المسكينة "

"I wonder who will put on your shoes for you now, dears?"

"أتساءل من سيرتدي حذائك من أجلك الآن ، أعزاء؟"

"and I wonder who will put on your stockings?"

"وأتساءل من سيرتدي جواربك؟"

"I shall be a great deal too far away"

"سأكون بعيدا جدا"

"I won't be able trouble myself about you anymore"

"لن أكون قادرا على إزعاج بشأنك بعد الآن"

Just at this moment her head struck against something

في هذه اللحظة فقط اصطدم رأسها بشيء ما

she had reached the roof of the hall

كانت قد وصلت إلى سطح القاعة

in fact, she was now more than two meters tall

في الواقع ، كان طولها الآن أكثر من مترين

and she at once took up the little golden key

وأخذت على الفور المفتاح الذهبي الصغير

and she hurried off to the garden door

وهرعت إلى باب الحديقة

Poor Alice! There was not much she could do

أليس المسكينة! لم يكن هناك الكثير الذي يمكنها فعله

she laid down on one side

استلقيت على جانب واحد

and she looked through into the garden with one eye

ونظرت إلى الحديقة بعين واحدة

but to get through was more hopeless than ever

لكن العبور كان ميؤوسا منه أكثر من أي وقت مضى

She sat down and began to cry again

جلست وبدأت في البكاء مرة أخرى

She went on shedding gallons of tears

واصلت ذرف جالونات من الدموع

soon there was a large pool all around her

سرعان ما كان هناك مسبح كبير حولها

and the water reached half-way down the hall

ووصل الماء إلى منتصف الطريق إلى أسفل القاعة

After a time, she heard a little pattering of feet

بعد فترة ، سمعت القليل من قعقعة القدمين

she heard the feet coming from the distance

سمعت القدمين قادمة من بعيد

and she hastily dried her eyes to see what was coming

وجففت عينيها على عجل لترى ما سيحدث

It was the White Rabbit returning

كان الأرنب الأبيض عائدا

he was splendidly dressed

كان يرتدي ملابس رائعة

he had a pair of white gloves in one hand

كان لديه زوج من القفازات البيضاء في يد واحدة

and he had a large feather fan in the other hand

وكان لديه مروحة كبيرة من الريش في اليد الأخرى

He came trotting along in a great hurry

جاء وهو يهرول في عجلة من أمره

and he muttered to himself, "Oh! the Duchess, the Duchess!"

وتمتم لنفسه ، "أوه! الدوقة ، الدوقة!"

"Oh! won't she be savage if I've kept her waiting!"

"أوه! ألن تكون متوحشة إذا أبقيتها تنتظر!

When the Rabbit came near her, Alice spoke

عندما اقترب منها الأرنب ، تحدثت أليس

but she spoke in a low, timid voice

لكنها تحدثت بصوت منخفض وخجول

"sir, please stop what you're doing for one moment"

"سيدي ، من فضلك توقف عما تفعله للحظة واحدة"

The Rabbit startled violently

أذهل الأرنب بعنف

he dropped the white gloves and the feather fan

أسقط القفازات البيضاء ومروحة الريش

and he scurried away into the darkness as fast as he could

واندفع بعيدا في الظلام بأسرع ما يمكن

Alice picked up the feather fan and gloves

التقطت أليس مروحة الريش والقفازات

and she kept fanning herself while she kept talking

واستمرت في تهوية نفسها بينما استمرت في الحديث

"Dear, dear! How strange everything is today!"

"عزيزتي ، عزيزي! كم هو غريب كل شيء اليوم!"

"yesterday things went on just as usual"

"بالأمس سارت الأمور كالمعتاد"

"Was I the same when I got up this morning?"

"هل كنت هو نفسه عندما استيقظت هذا الصباح؟"

"But if I'm not the same, there is another question"

"ولكن إذا لم أكن هو نفسه ، فهناك سؤال آخر"

"Who in the world am I?"

"من في العالم أنا؟"

"Ah, that's the great puzzle!"

"آه ، هذا هو اللغز العظيم!"

As she said this, she looked down at her hands

عندما قالت هذا ، نظرت إلى يديها

she was wearing one of the rabbits little white gloves

كانت ترتدي أحد القفازات البيضاء الصغيرة للأرانب

she hadn't noticed she put the glove on while talking

لم تلاحظ أنها ارتدت القفاز أثناء التحدث

"How can I have done that?" she thought

"كيف يمكنني أن أفعل ذلك؟" فكرت

"I must be growing small again"

"يجب أن أكون صغيرا مرة أخرى"

She got up and went to the table to measure her height

نهضت وذهبت إلى الطاولة لقياس طولها

she found that she was now about half a meter tall

وجدت أنها الآن يبلغ طولها حوالي نصف متر

and she was still shrinking rapidly

وكانت لا تزال تتقلص بسرعة

She soon found out what the cause of the shrinking was

سرعان ما اكتشفت سبب الانكماش

the feather fan was making her smaller again!

كانت مروحة الريش تجعلها أصغر مرة أخرى!

and she dropped the feather fan hastily

وأسقطت مروحة الريشة على عجل

she dropped the feather fan just in time to save herself

أسقطت مروحة الريشة في الوقت المناسب لإنقاذ نفسها

had she fanned herself any longer she would have shrunk
away entirely

لو كانت تهوية نفسها بعد الآن لكانت قد تقلصت تماما

"That was a narrow escape!" said Alice

"كان ذلك هروبا ضيقا!" قالت أليس

and she was a good deal frightened at the sudden change

وكانت خائفة كثيرا من التغيير المفاجئ

but she was very glad to find herself still in existence

لكنها كانت سعيدة جدا لتجد نفسها لا تزال موجودة

"And now, off to the garden!"

"والآن ، انطلق إلى الحديقة!"

And she ran with all speed back to the little door

وركضت بكل سرعة عائدة إلى الباب الصغير

but, alas! the little door was shut again

لكن ، للأسف! تم إغلاق الباب الصغير مرة أخرى

and the little golden key was lying on the glass table again

وكان المفتاح الذهبي الصغير مستلقيا على الطاولة الزجاجية مرة أخرى

"Things are worse than ever," thought the poor child

"الأمور أسوأ من أي وقت مضى" ، فكر الطفل المسكين

"I never was so small as this before, never!"

"لم أكن أبدا صغيرا مثل هذا من قبل ، أبدا!"

As she said these words, her foot slipped

عندما قالت هذه الكلمات ، انزلقت قدمها

and in another moment there was a great splash!

وفي لحظة أخرى كان هناك دفقة كبيرة!

she was up to her chin in salt-water

كانت تصل إلى ذقنها في الماء المالح

Her first idea was that she had somehow fallen into the sea

كانت فكرتها الأولى هي أنها سقطت بطريقة ما في البحر

However, she soon realized what she was in

ومع ذلك ، سرعان ما أدركت ما كانت فيه

she was in a pool of tears

كانت في بركة من الدموع

the tears she had wept when she was two meters tall

الدموع التي بكت عندما كان طولها مترين

Just then she heard something

عندها فقط سمعت شيئا

something was splashing about in the pool

كان هناك شيء يتناثر في المسبح

the splashing came from a little way off

جاء الرش من بعيد قليلا

and she swam nearer to see what the splashing was

وسبحت بالقرب لترى ما هو الرش

she soon saw that it was only a little mouse

سرعان ما رأت أنه كان مجرد فأر صغير

the little mouse had slipped in to the water too

انزلق الفأر الصغير إلى الماء أيضا

Alice thought to herself about the situation

فكرت أليس في نفسها في الموقف

"Would it be of any use to speak to this mouse?"

"هل سيكون من المفيد التحدث إلى هذا الفأر؟"

"Everything is so up-side-down down here"

"كل شيء مقلوب للغاية هنا"

"I should think very likely this mouse can talk"

"يجب أن أعتقد على الأرجح أن هذا الفأر يمكنه التحدث"

"at any rate, there's no harm in trying"

"على أي حال ، لا ضرر من المحاولة"

So she began trying to talk to the mouse

لذلك بدأت تحاول التحدث إلى الفأر

"Oh Mouse, do you know the way out of this pool?"

"يا فأر ، هل تعرف طريقة الخروج من هذا البركة؟"

"I am very tired of swimming about here, Oh Mouse!"

"لقد سئمت جدا من السباحة هنا ، يا فأر!"

The mouse looked at her rather inquisitively

نظر إليها الفأر بفضول إلى حد ما

the mouse seemed to wink with one of its little eyes

بدا أن الفأر يغمز بإحدى عينيه الصغيرتين

but the little mouse said nothing

لكن الفأر الصغير لم يقل شيئا

"Perhaps the mouse doesn't understand English," thought Alice

"ربما الفأر لا يفهم اللغة الإنجليزية" ، فكرت أليس

"I dare say it's a French mouse"

"أجرؤ على القول إنه فأر فرنسي"

"perhaps this mouse came over with William the Conqueror"

"ربما جاء هذا الفأر مع ويليام الفاتح"

So she began again, in French

لذلك بدأت مرة أخرى باللغة الفرنسية

"Where is my cat?" she asked in French

"أين قطتي؟" سألت بالفرنسية

it was the first sentence in her French lesson-book

كانت الجملة الأولى في كتاب دروس اللغة الفرنسية

The Mouse gave a sudden leap out of the water

قفز الفأر فجأة من الماء

and the mouse seemed to quiver all over with fright

وبدا أن الفأر يرتجف في كل مكان من الخوف

"Oh, I beg your pardon!" cried Alice hastily

"أوه ، أطلب العفو!" صرخت أليس على عجل

she was afraid that she had hurt the poor animal's feelings

كانت خائفة من أنها قد جرحت مشاعر المسكين

"I quite forgot you didn't like cats"

"لقد نسيت تماما أنك لا تحب القطط"

"I don't like cats!" cried the Mouse in a shrill, passionate voice

"أنا لا أحب القطط!" صرخ الفأر بصوت حاد وعاطفي

"Would you like cats, if you were me?"

"هل تريد القطط ، إذا كنت أنا؟"

Alice comforted the mouse in a soothing tone

أراحت أليس الماوس بنبرة مهدئة

"Well, perhaps I would not like cats if I were you either"

"حسنا ، ربما لا أحب القطط إذا كنت مكانك أيضا"

"please don't be angry about the mention of cats"

"من فضلك لا تغضب من ذكر القطط"

"And yet I wish I could show you our cat Dinah"

"ومع ذلك أتمنى أن أريك قطتنا دينا"

"if you met her I think you'd take a fancy to cats"

"إذا قابلتها ، أعتقد أنك ستتخيل القطط"

"if you could only see her"

"إذا كان بإمكانك رؤيتها فقط"

"She is such a dear, quiet thing"

"إنها شيء عزيز وهادئ"

The mouse was shaking all over

كان الفأر يرتجف في كل مكان

Alice felt certain the mouse must be really offended

شعرت أليس بالتأكد من أن الفأر يجب أن يشعر بالإهانة حقا

"We won't talk about her any more, if you'd rather not"

"لن نتحدث عنها بعد الآن ، إذا كنت تفضل عدم ذلك"

"We, indeed!" cried the Mouse

"نحن ، حقا!" صرخ الفأر

the mouse was trembling down to the end of its tail

كان الفأر يرتجف حتى نهاية ذيله

"As if I would talk on such a subject!"

"كما لو كنت سأتحدث عن مثل هذا الموضوع!"

"Our family always hated cats"

"عائلتنا تكره القطط دائما"

"cats; nasty, low, vulgar things!"

"القطط. أشياء سيئة ، منخفضة ، مبتذلة!"

"Don't let me hear the name again!"

"لا تدعني أسمع الاسم مرة أخرى!"

"I won't mention cats again indeed!" said Alice

"لن أذكر القطط مرة أخرى بالفعل!" قالت أليس

she was in a great hurry to change the subject

كانت في عجلة من أمرها لتغيير الموضوع

"Are you... are you fond of dogs?"

"هل أنت ... هل أنت مغرم بالكلاب؟

"There is such a nice little dog near our house,"

"هناك مثل هذا الصغير اللطيف بالقرب من منزلنا ،"

"I should like to show you the little dog!"

"أود أن أريك الصغير!"

"this little dog kills all the rats and...

"هذا الصغير يقتل كل الفئران و ...

"oh, dear!" cried Alice in a sorrowful tone

"أوه ، عزيزي!" صرخت أليس بنبرة حزينة

"I'm afraid I've offended you again!"

"أخشى أنني أساءت إليك مرة أخرى!"

the mouse was swimming away from her as fast as it could go

كان الفأر يسبح بعيدا عنها بأسرع ما يمكن أن يذهب

and the mouse made quite a commotion in the pool

وأثار الفأر ضجة كبيرة في المسبح

So she called softly after the mouse

لذلك اتصلت بهدوء بعد الفأر

"my dear mouse, please come back!"

"عزيزي الفأر ، من فضلك عد!"

"and we won't talk about cats"

"ولن نتحدث عن القطط"

"and we don't have to talk about dogs either"

"وليس علينا التحدث عن أيضا"

When the mouse heard this, it turned around

عندما سمع الفأر هذا ، استدار

and the little mouse swam slowly back to her

وسبح الفأر الصغير ببطء عائدا إليها

the mouse's face was quite pale

كان وجه الفأر شاحبا جدا

and the mouse spoke, in a low, trembling voice

وتحدث الفأر بصوت منخفض يرتجف

"Let us get to the shore"

"دعونا نصل إلى الشاطئ"

"and then I'll tell you my history"

"وبعد ذلك سأخبرك بتاريخي"

"and you'll understand why it is I hate cats and dogs"

"وستفهم لماذا أكره القطط"

It had become high time to go

لقد حان الوقت للذهاب

because the pool was getting quite crowded

لأن المسبح كان مزدحما للغاية

other birds and animals had fallen into the pool

سقطت طيور أخرى في البركة

there were a Duck and a Dodo

كان هناك بطة ودودو

and there was a Lory bird and an Eaglet

وكان هناك طائر لوري ونسر

and there were several other interesting looking creatures

وكان هناك العديد من المخلوقات الأخرى ذات المظهر المثير للاهتمام

Alice led the way out the pool

قادت أليس الطريق للخروج من المسبح

and the whole party of animals swam to the shore

وسبحت مجموعة بأكملها إلى الشاطئ

A caucus race and a long tail
سباق حزبي وذيل طويل

They were indeed a funny-looking bunch of animals

لقد كانوا بالفعل مجموعة من ذات المظهر المضحك

and they all assembled on the water's bank

وتجمعوا جميعا على ضفة المياه

the birds all had bedraggled feathers

كانت جميع الطيور لديها ريش ممزق

and the furry animals were soaked through

وغارقة ذات الفراء

and all were dripping wet, annoyed and uncomfortable

وكان الجميع يقطر مبللة ومنزعجة وغير مريحة

there was one question that had to be answered first

كان هناك سؤال واحد يجب الإجابة عليه أولا

what is the best way for everyone to get dry?

ما هي أفضل طريقة للجميع للجفاف؟

They had a consultation about this matter

لقد أجروا مشاورات حول هذا الأمر

soon they were all on familiar terms

سرعان ما أصبحوا جميعا على شروط مألوفة

it was as if she had known them all her life

كان الأمر كما لو كانت تعرفهم طوال حياتها

the mouse seemed to be a person of some authority

بدا الفأر وكأنه شخص يتمتع ببعض السلطة

"Sit down, all of you, and listen to me!

"اجلس ، جميعكم ، واستمعوا إلي!"

"I'll soon make you all dry again!"

"سأجعلكم جميعا تجففون قريبا مرة أخرى!"

They all sat down at once, in a large ring

جلسوا جميعا في وقت واحد ، في حلقة كبيرة

and the little mouse sat in the middle

وجلس الفأر الصغير في المنتصف

"Ahem!" said the mouse with an important air

"مهم!" قال الفأر بهواء مهم

"Are you all ready?"

"هل أنتم مستعدون تماما؟"

"This is the driest thing I know"

"هذا هو أكثر الأشياء جفافا التي أعرفها"

"Silence all around, if you please!"

"الصمت في كل مكان ، إذا سمحت!"

"William the Conqueror was favoured by the pope"

"كان وليام الفاتح مفضلا من قبل البابا"

"but he was soon submitted to by the English"

"لكنه سرعان ما خضع له الإنجليز"

"they wanted leaders of late"

"لقد أرادوا قادة في الآونة الأخيرة"

"and they had been accustomed to power and conquest"

"وقد اعتادوا على السلطة والغزو"

"Edwin and Morcar, the Earls of Mercia and Northumbria"

"إدوين وموركار ، إيرل ميرسيا ونورثمبريا"

"Ugh!" said the lori bird, with a shiver

"قرف!" قال طائر لوري برعشة

"and even Stigand, the patriotic archbishop of Canterbury"

"وحتى ستيجاند ، رئيس أساقفة كانتربري الوطني"

"he also found it advisable"

"وجد ذلك مستصوبا أيضا"

"What did he find advisable?" said the duck

"ما الذي وجد أنه مستحسن؟" قالت البطة

"He found it advisable" the mouse replied rather crossly

"لقد وجد أنه من المستحسن ذلك" أجاب الفأر بغضب إلى حد ما

but the duck was not satisfied

لكن البطة لم تكن راضية

"of course, you know what 'it' means"

"بالطبع ، أنت تعرف ما تعنيه" إنها """

"I know what 'it' is when I find a thing," said the duck

قالت البطة: "أعرف ما هو" عندما أجد شيئا ما

"it's generally a frog or a worm"

"إنه بشكل عام ضفدع أو دودة"

"The question is, what did the archbishop find?"

"السؤال هو ، ماذا وجد رئيس الأساقفة؟"

The mouse did not notice this question

لم يلاحظ الفأر هذا السؤال

instead, the mouse hurriedly went on with the speech

بدلا من ذلك ، واصل الفأر على عجل الخطاب

"he found it advisable to go with Edgar Atheling"

"وجد أنه من المستحسن الذهاب مع إدغار أثيلينج"

"to meet William and offer him the crown"

"لمقابلة ويليام وتقديم التاج له"

the mouse continued, turning to Alice as it spoke

واصل الفأر ، متفت إلى أليس وهو يتحدث

"How are you getting on now, my dear?"

"كيف حالك الآن يا عزيزي؟"

"As wet as ever," said Alice in a melancholy tone

"مبللة أكثر من أي وقت مضى" ، قالت أليس بنبرة حزينة

"this story doesn't seem to dry me at all"

"لا يبدو أن هذه القصة تجففني على الإطلاق"

"In that case," said the dodo solemnly, rising to its feet

"في هذه الحالة" ، قال الدودو رسميا ، وهو يقف على قدميه

"I vote that the meeting be adjourned"

"أصوت على تأجيل الجلسة"

"and I propose an immediate adoption of more energetic remedies"

"وأقترح الاعتماد الفوري لعلاجات أكثر نشاطا"

"Speak real words!" said the eaglet

"تحدث بكلمات حقيقية!" قال النسر

"I don't know the meaning of half of those long words"

"لا أعرف معنى نصف تلك الكلمات الطويلة"

"and, what's more, I don't believe you know either!"

"والأكثر من ذلك ، لا أعتقد أنك تعرف أيضا!"

"What I was going to say," said the dodo in an offended tone

"ما كنت سأقوله" ، قال طائر الدودو بنبرة مستاءة

"the best thing to get us dry would be a caucus-race"

"أفضل شيء لجعلنا يجففون هو سباق المؤتمر"

"What is a caucus-race?" said Alice

"ما هو سباق المؤتمرات الحزبية؟" قالت أليس

"Well," said the dodo, "the best way to explain it is to do it"

قال طائر الدودو: "حسنا ، أفضل طريقة لشرح ذلك هي القيام بذلك"

"First the dodo marked out a race-course"

"أولا ، حدد طائر الدودو مضمار سباق"

"the track was in a sort of circle"

"كان المسار في نوع من الدائرة"

"and then all the party were placed along the course"

"ثم تم وضع كل الحفلة على طول المسار"

There was no "One, two, three and away!"

لم يكن هناك "واحد ، اثنان ، ثلاثة وبعيدا!"

but they began running when they liked

لكنهم بدأوا في الركض عندما يحبون

and they also finished when they liked

وانتهوا أيضا عندما أحلو لهم
so it was not easy to know when the race was over
لذلك لم يكن من السهل معرفة متى انتهى السباق
after half an hour or so of running they were all quite dry
بعد نصف ساعة أو نحو ذلك من الجري ، كانوا جميعا جافين تماما
the dodo suddenly called out, "The race is over!"
صرخ طائر الدودو فجأة ، "انتهى السباق!"
and they all crowded around the dodo
واحتشدوا جميعا حول طائر الدودو
all the animals were panting and puffing
كانت جميع تلهث وتنتفخ
and they all wanted to know, "But who has won?"
وأرادوا جميعا أن يعرفوا ، "لكن من فاز؟"
This question the dodo could not immediately answer
لم يستطع طائر الدودو الإجابة على هذا السؤال على الفور
first he had to do a great deal of thinking
أولا كان عليه أن يفكر كثيرا
after much thinking, the dodo finally spoke
بعد الكثير من التفكير ، تحدث طائر الدودو أخيرا
"Everybody has won, and all must have prizes"
"لقد فاز الجميع ، ويجب أن يحصل الجميع على جوائز"
"But who is to give the prizes?" asked a chorus of voices
"لكن من سيعطي الجوائز؟" سألت جوقة من الأصوات
"Well, she, of course," said the dodo
"حسنا ، هي ، بالطبع"، قال طائر الدودو
and the dodo pointed with one finger to Alice
وأشار طائر الدودو بإصبع واحد إلى أليس
and the whole party of animals crowded around her
ومجموعة بأكملها مزدحمة حولها
they called out, in a confused way, "Prizes! Prizes!"
نادوا بطريقة مرتبكة ، "الجوائز! الجوائز!"
Alice had no idea what to do
لم يكن لدى أليس أي فكرة عما يجب القيام به
in despair she put her hand into her pocket
في حالة من اليأس وضعت يدها في جيبها
and she pulled out a box of sweets

وسحبت علبة حلويات
luckily the salt-water had not got into the box
لحسن الحظ ، لم تدخل المياه المالحة في الصندوق
and she handed the sweets around as prizes
وسلمت الحلويات كجوائز
There was exactly one piece for everyone
كان هناك قطعة واحدة بالضبط للجميع
The next thing they had to do was to eat the sweets
الشيء التالي الذي كان عليهم فعله هو تناول الحلويات
this caused some noise and confusion
تسبب هذا في بعض الضوضاء والارتباك
the large birds complained that they could not taste their sweets
اشتكت الطيور الكبيرة من أنها لا تستطيع تذوق حلوياتها
the small ones choked and had to be patted on the back
اختنق الصغار وكان لا بد من التربيت على ظهورهم
However, it was over at last
ومع ذلك ، انتهى الأمر أخيرا
and they sat down again in a ring
وجلسوا مرة أخرى في حلقة
and they begged the mouse to tell them something more
وتوسلوا إلى الفأر أن يخبرهم بشيء أكثر
"You promised to tell me your history, you know," said Alice
قالت أليس "لقد وعدت أن تخبرني بتاريخك ، كما تعلم"
and she made another little remark about cats in a whisper
وأدلت بملاحظة صغيرة أخرى عن القطط في همس
she didn't want to offend the mouse again
لم تكن تريد الإساءة إلى الفأر مرة أخرى
the little mouse turned to Alice and sighed
التفت الفأر الصغير إلى أليس وتنهد
"Mine is a long and a sad tale!"
"حكايتي طويلة وحزينة!"
"It is a long tail, certainly," said Alice
قالت أليس "إنه ذيل طويل بالتأكيد"
and she looked down with wonder at the mouse's tail
ونظرت إلى الأسفل بدهشة إلى ذيل الفأر

"but why do you call it a sad tail?"

"لكن لماذا تسميها ذيلا حزينا؟"

And she kept on puzzling about it while the mouse was speaking

واستمرت في الحيرة حيال ذلك بينما كان الفأر يتحدث

so that her idea of the tale was something like this

بحيث كانت فكرتها عن الحكاية شيئا من هذا القبيل

```
        "Fury said to
           a mouse, That
              he met in the
                 house, 'Let
                    us both go
                      to law: I
                         will prosecute
                      you.—
                         Come, I'll
                      take no denial:
                   We must have
                the trial;
                For really
             this morning
         I've
       nothing
     to do.'
           Said the
              mouse to
                 the cur,
                   'Such a
                     trial, dear
                       sir, With
                          no jury
                            or judge,
                              would
                            be wasting
                              our
                    breath.'
                   'I'll be
                 judge,
              I'll be
          jury,'
        said
      cunning
         old
            Fury;
               'I'll
                  try
                    the
                      whole
                        cause,
                        and
                       condemn
                      you to
            death.'"
```

Fury said to a mouse, That he met in the house"

" قال الغضب للفأر ، إنه التقى في المنزل

Let us both go to law: I will prosecute you

دعونا نذهب إلى القانون: سأحاكمك

Come, I'll take no denial: We must have the trial

تعال ، لن أقبل أي إنكار: يجب أن نحصل على المحاكمة

For really this morning I've nothing to do

حقا هذا الصباح ليس لدي ما أفعله

Said the mouse to the cur;

قال الفأر للكير.

Such a trial, dear sir, With no jury or judge, would be wasting our breath

مثل هذه المحاكمة ، سيدي العزيز ، بدون هيئة محلفين أو قاض ، ستضيع أنفاسنا

"I'll be judge, I'll be jury," said cunning old Fury

"سأكون قاضيا ، سأكون هيئة محلفين" ، قال فيوري العجوز الماكر

I'll try the whole cause, and condemn you to death

سأجرب القضية برمتها ، وأحكم عليك بالموت

the mouse spoke severely to Alice

تحدث الفأر بشدة إلى أليس

"You are not paying attention!"

"أنت لا تنتبه!"

"What are you thinking of?"

"ما الذي تفكر فيه؟"

"I beg your pardon," said Alice very humbly

"أطلب العفو" ، قالت أليس بتواضع شديد

"you had got to the fifth bend, I think?"

"لقد وصلت إلى المنعطف الخامس ، على ما أعتقد؟"

"You insult me by talking such nonsense!"

"أنت تهينني بالكلام بمثل هذا الهراء!"

and the mouse got up and walked away

ونهض الفأر وابتعد

Alice called after the little mouse

اتصلت أليس بالفأر الصغير

"Please come back and finish your story!"

"من فضلك عد وقم بإنهاء قصتك!"

And the others all joined in chorus

وانضم الآخرون جميعا في الجوقة

"Yes, please do finish your story!"

"نعم ، من فضلك قم بإنهاء قصتك!"

But the mouse only shook its head impatiently

لكن الفأر هز رأسه بفارغ الصبر فقط

and the little mouse walked a little quicker

ومشى الفأر الصغير أسرع قليلا

"I wish I had Dinah, our cat, here!" said Alice

"أتمنى لو كان لدي دينا ، قطتنا ، هنا!" قالت أليس

This caused a remarkable sensation among the party

تسبب هذا في ضجة كبيرة بين الحزب

Some of the birds hurried off at once

سارعت بعض الطيور في الحال

and a Canary called out in a trembling voice, to its children;

ونادى الكناري بصوت مرتجف لأطفاله.

"Come away, my dears!"

"تعال بعيدا يا أعزائي!"

"It's high time you were all in bed!"

"لقد حان الوقت لتكون جميعا في السرير!"

with various excuses they all went away

بأعذار مختلفة ذهبوا جميعا بعيدا

and Alice was soon left alone

وسرعان ما تركت أليس بمفردها

"I wish I hadn't mentioned Dinah!"

"أتمنى لو لم أذكر دينا!"

"Nobody seems to like her down here"

"لا يبدو أن أحدا يحبها هنا"

"but I'm sure she's the best cat in the world!"

"لكنني متأكد من أنها أفضل قطة في العالم!"

Poor Alice began to cry again

بدأت أليس المسكينة في البكاء مرة أخرى

because she felt very lonely and low-spirited

لأنها شعرت بالوحدة الشديدة والروح المنخفضة

In a little while, however, she again heard something

ومع ذلك ، في فترة وجيزة ، سمعت شيئا مرة أخرى

a little pattering of footsteps in the distance

القليل من خطى الخطى في المسافة

and she looked up eagerly

ونظرت بفارغ الصبر

The rabbit sends in little Mr Bill
الأرنب يرسل السيد بيل الصغير

It was the white rabbit,trotting slowly back again

كان الأرنب الأبيض ، يهرول ببطء مرة أخرى

he was looking about anxiously as he went

كان ينظر بقلق وهو يذهب

he looked as if he had lost something

بدا كما لو أنه فقد شيئا ما

Alice heard him muttering to himself

سمعته أليس يتمتم لنفسه

"The Duchess! The Duchess! Oh, my dear paws!"

"الدوقة! الدوقة! أوه ، كفوفي العزيزة!

"Oh, my fur and whiskers!"

"أوه ، فروي وشعيراتي!"

"She'll get me executed, I'm sure of that"

"ستعدني ، أنا متأكد من ذلك"

"just as sure as ferrets are ferrets!"

"تماما مثل القوارض هي قوارض!"

"Where can I have dropped my things, I wonder?"

"أين يمكنني أن أسقط أغراضي ، أتساءل؟"

Alice guessed in a moment what he was looking for

خمنت أليس في لحظة ما كان يبحث عنه

he was looking for the feather fan

كان يبحث عن مروحة الريشة

and he was looking for the pair of white gloves

وكان يبحث عن زوج من القفازات البيضاء

so she very good-naturedly began looking for the gloves

لذلك بدأت بلطف شديد في البحث عن القفازات

and she looked for the feather fan too

وبحثت عن مروحة الريشة أيضا

but the gloves and feather fan were nowhere to be seen

لكن القفازات ومروحة الريش لم تكن مرئية في أي مكان

everything seemed to have changed since her swim in the pool

يبدو أن كل شيء قد تغير منذ أن سبحت في المسبح

nothing was the same since she had been in the great hall

لم يكن هناك شيء كما هو منذ أن كانت في القاعة الكبرى

and the glass table had vanished

واختفت الطاولة الزجاجية

and the little door wasn't there either

ولم يكن الباب الصغير موجودا أيضا

Very soon the rabbit noticed Alice

سرعان ما لاحظ الأرنب أليس

he called to her in an angry tone

ناداها بنبرة غاضبة

"Mary Ann, what are you doing out here?"

"ماري آن ، ماذا تفعل هنا؟"

"Run home this moment"

"اركض إلى المنزل هذه اللحظة"

"and fetch me a pair of gloves and a feather fan!"

"وأحضر لي زوجا من القفازات ومروحة ريش!"

"and be quick about it!"

"وكن سريعا في ذلك!"

Alice spoke to herself as she ran off

تحدثت أليس إلى نفسها وهي تهرب

"He must have mistaken me for his housemaid!"

"لا بد أنه أخطأ في أنني خادمة منزله!"

"How surprised he'll be when he finds out who I am!"

"كم سيكون مندهشا عندما يكتشف من أنا!"

As she said this, she came upon a neat little house

عندما قالت هذا ، صادفت منزلا صغيرا أنيقا

on the door of the house was a bright brass plate

على باب المنزل كان هناك صفيحة نحاسية لامعة

"W. RABBIT"

"دبليو أرنب"

She went in without knocking on the door

دخلت دون أن تطرق الباب

and she hurried straight upstairs

وسارعت مباشرة إلى الطابق العلوي

she worried that she might meet the real Mary Ann

كانت قلقة من أنها قد تلتقي بماري آن الحقيقية

because then she would be turned out of the house

لأنه بعد ذلك سيتم إخراجها من المنزل

and she wouldn't be able to find the feather fan and gloves

ولن تتمكن من العثور على مروحة الريش والقفازات

Alice had found her way into a tidy little room

وجدت أليس طريقها إلى غرفة صغيرة مرتبة

in the room was a table by the window

في الغرفة كانت هناك طاولة بجانب النافذة

and on the table was a feather fan

وعلى الطاولة كان هناك مروحة من الريش

and there were two or three pairs of tiny white gloves

وكان هناك زوجان أو ثلاثة أزواج من القفازات البيضاء الصغيرة

she picked up the feather fan and a pair of the gloves

التقطت مروحة الريش وزوج من القفازات

and she was just about to leave the room

وكانت على وشك مغادرة الغرفة

but then her eyes fell upon a little bottle

ولكن بعد ذلك سقطت عيناها على زجاجة صغيرة

She uncorked the bottle and put it to her lips

فكت الزجاجة ووضعتها على شفتيها

"I do hope it'll make me grow large again"

"آمل أن يجعلني أنمو بشكل كبير مرة أخرى"

"I'm tired of being such a tiny little thing!"

"لقد سئمت من أن أكون شيئا صغيرا!"

Alice had hardly drunk half the bottle

بالكاد شربت أليس نصف الزجاجة

her head was already pressing against the ceiling

كان رأسها يضغط بالفعل على السقف

and she had to stoop down

وكان عليها أن تنحني

to save her neck from being broken

لإنقاذ رقبتها من الكسر

She hastily put down the bottle

وضعت الزجاجة على عجل

"That's quite enough"

"هذا يكفي تماما"

"I hope I don't grow anymore"

"آمل ألا أنمو بعد الآن"

Alas! It was too late to wish that!

واحسرتاه! لقد فات الأوان لأتمنى ذلك!

She went on growing and growing

استمرت في النمو والنمو

and very soon she had to kneel down on the floor

وسرعان ما اضطرت إلى الركوع على الأرض

and even then she went on growing

وحتى ذلك الحين استمرت في النمو

as a last resource she put one arm out of the window

كمورد أخير ، وضعت ذراعا واحدة من النافذة

and she put one foot up the chimney

ووضعت قدما واحدة فوق المدخنة

"Now I can do no more, whatever happens"

"الآن لا يمكنني فعل المزيد، مهما حدث"

"What will become of me?"

"ماذا سيحدث لي؟"

Alice had a spot of luck

كان لدى أليس بقعة حظ

the little magic bottle had had its full effect

كان للزجاجة السحرية الصغيرة تأثيرها الكامل

and Alice grew no larger than she was

ولم تنمو أليس أكبر مما كانت عليه

After a few minutes she heard a voice outside

بعد بضع دقائق سمعت صوتا في الخارج

and she stopped to listen to the voice

وتوقفت للاستماع إلى الصوت

"Mary Ann! Mary Ann!" said the voice

"ماري آن! ماري آن!" قال الصوت

"Fetch me my gloves this moment!"

"أحضر لي قفازاتي هذه اللحظة!"

Then came a little pattering of feet on the stairs

ثم جاء القليل من الأقدام على الدرج

Alice knew it was the rabbit coming to look for her

عرفت أليس أن الأرنب قادم للبحث عنها

and she trembled till she shook the house

وارتجفت حتى هزت المنزل

she quite forgot what her proportions were

لقد نسيت تماما ما هي نسبها

she was a thousand times as large as the rabbit

كانت أكبر بألف مرة من الأرنب

and she had no reason to be afraid of a rabbit

ولم يكن لديها سبب للخوف من الأرنب

Presently the rabbit came up to the door

في الوقت الحاضر صعد الأرنب إلى الباب

and the little rabbit tried to open the door

وحاول الأرنب الصغير فتح الباب

the door started to open inwards

بدأ الباب يفتح إلى الداخل

but Alice's elbow was pressed hard against the door

لكن مرفق أليس تم الضغط عليه بقوة على الباب

that attempt proved a failure

أثبتت هذه المحاولة فشلها

Alice heard the rabbit speak to himself

سمعت أليس الأرنب يتحدث إلى نفسه

"Then I'll go around and get in through the window"

"ثم سأتجول وأدخل من النافذة"

"That you won't!" thought Alice

"لن تفعل!" فكرت أليس

and she waited a little again

وانتظرت قليلا مرة أخرى

soon she heard the rabbit just under the window

سرعان ما سمعت الأرنب تحت النافذة مباشرة

she suddenly spread out her hand

فجأة مدت يدها

and she made a snatch in the air

وقامت بخطف في الهواء

She did not get hold of anything

لم تحصل على أي شيء

but she heard a little shriek and a fall

لكنها سمعت صراخا صغيرا وسقوطا

and she heard a crash of broken glass

وسمعت تحطم الزجاج المكسور

perhaps the rabbit had fallen

ربما سقط الأرنب

maybe he was in a green-house

ربما كان في دفيئة

Next came an angry voice; the rabbit's voice

بعد ذلك جاء صوت غاضب. صوت الأرنب

"Pat, where are you?"

"بات ، أين أنت؟"

And then came a voice she had never heard before

ثم جاء صوت لم تسمعه من قبل

"your honour, I'm here!"

"شرفك ، أنا هنا!"

"I'm digging for apples"

"أنا أحفر بحثا عن التفاح"

"Here! Come and help me out of this!"

"هنا! تعال وساعدني على الخروج من هذا!"

"Now tell me, Pat, what's that in the window?"

"الآن قل لي يا بات ، ما هذا في النافذة؟"

"Sure, your honour, I will tell you"

"بالتأكيد ، حضرتك ، سأخبرك"

"it's an arm that's in the window!"

"إنها ذراع في النافذة!"

"Well, an arm has no business there"

"حسنا ، الذراع ليس لها عمل هناك"

"go and take the arm away!"

"اذهب وخذ الذراع بعيدا!"

There was a long silence after this

ساد صمت طويل بعد ذلك

and Alice could only hear whispers now and then

ولم تستطع أليس سماع الهمسات إلا بين الحين والآخر

and at last she spread out her hand again

وأخيرا مدت يدها مرة أخرى

and she made another snatch in the air

وقامت بانتزاع آخر في الهواء

This time there were two little shrieks

هذه المرة كان هناك صرختان صغيرتان

and there was more sounds of broken glass

وكان هناك المزيد من أصوات الزجاج المكسور

"I wonder what they'll do next!" thought Alice

"أتساءل ماذا سيفعلون بعد ذلك!" فكرت أليس

"I wish they would pull me out the window"

"أتمنى أن يسحبوني من النافذة"

She waited for some time

انتظرت لبعض الوقت

but for a while she didn't hear anything more

لكن لفترة من الوقت لم تسمع أي شيء آخر

At last came a rumbling of little wheels

أخيرا جاء قعقعة من العجلات الصغيرة

and there came the sound of a good many voices

وجاء صوت أصوات كثيرة

all the voices were talking together

كانت كل الأصوات تتحدث معا

She could make out some of the words

يمكنها أن تصنع بعض الكلمات

"Where's the other ladder?"

"أين السلم الآخر؟"

"Bill's got the other ladder"

"بيل لديه السلم الآخر"

"Bill, come here!"

"بيل ، تعال إلى هنا!"

"Will the roof bear the load?"

"هل سيتحمل السقف العبء؟"

"Who wants to go down the chimney?"

"من يريد أن ينزل المدخنة؟"

"Nay, I shall not! You do it!"

"لا ، لن أفعل! أنت تفعل ذلك!"

"Here, Bill!"

"هنا يا بيل!"

"The master says you've got to go down the chimney!"

"يقول السيد إنه يجب عليك النزول من المدخنة!"

Alice drew her foot as far down the chimney as she could

سحبت أليس قدمها إلى أسفل المدخنة قدر استطاعتها

and then she waited to see what was coming

ثم انتظرت لترى ما سيحدث

she heard a little animal scratching and scrambling

سمعت صغيرا يخدش ويتدافع

the little animal must be in the chimney

يجب أن يكون الصغير في المدخنة

then she gave one sharp kick

ثم أطلقت ركلة حادة واحدة

and she waited to see what would happen next

وانتظرت لترى ما سيحدث بعد ذلك

she heard a general chorus of voices

سمعت جوقة عامة من الأصوات

"There goes Bill!" they all said

"ها هو بيل!" قالوا جميعا

then she heard the rabbit's voice alone

ثم سمعت صوت الأرنب وحده

"You by the hedge, catch him!"

"أنت بجانب السياج ، أمسك به!"

there was another moment of silence

كانت هناك لحظة صمت أخرى

and then there was another confusion of voices

ثم كان هناك ارتباك آخر في الأصوات

"Hold up his head, Brandy"

"ارفع رأسه يا براندي"

"be careful not to choke him"

"احرص على عدم خنقه"

"What happened to you?"

"ماذا حدث لك؟"

Last came a little feeble, squeaking voice

جاء آخر صوت ضعيف قليلا وصرير

"Well, I hardly know no more"

"حسنا ، بالكاد لا أعرف المزيد"

"thank you all, I'm better now"

"شكرا لكم جميعا ، أنا أفضل الآن"

"there is one thing I can remember"

"هناك شيء واحد يمكنني تذكره"

"something comes at me like a train in a tunnel"

"شيء ما يأتي إلي مثل قطار في نفق"

"and up I fly like a sky-rocket!"

"وأنا أطير مثل صاروخ السماء!"

there was a minute or two of silence

سادت دقيقة أو دقيقتين من الصمت

and then they began moving about again

ثم بدأوا في التحرك مرة أخرى

and Alice heard the Rabbit speak again

وسمعت أليس الأرنب يتحدث مرة أخرى

"A barrowful will do, to begin with"

"العربة سوف تفعل ، في البداية"

"A barrowful of what?" thought Alice

"عربة مليئة بماذا؟" فكرت أليس

But she was not kept in suspense for long

لكنها لم تبقى في حالة تشويق لفترة طويلة

a shower of little pebbles came through the window

جاء وابل من الحصى الصغيرة من خلال النافذة

and some of the little pebbles hit her in the face

وضربتها بعض الحصى الصغيرة في وجهها

Alice was surprised about the little pebbles

فوجئت أليس بالحصى الصغيرة

all the little pebbles were turning into cakes

كل الحصى الصغيرة كانت تتحول إلى كعك

and a bright idea came into her head

وجاءت فكرة مشرقة في رأسها

"I should eat one of these cakes"

"يجب أن آكل واحدة من هذه الكعكات"

"cake is sure to make some change in my size"

"من المؤكد أن الكعكة ستحدث بعض التغيير في حجمي"

So she swallowed one of the cakes

لذلك ابتلعت إحدى الكعك

and she was delighted to find that she began shrinking

وكانت سعيدة عندما وجدت أنها بدأت في الانكماش

soon she was small enough to get through the door

سرعان ما أصبحت صغيرة بما يكفي لعبور الباب

she ran out of the house

ركضت من المنزل

a crowd of little animals and birds were waiting outside

كان حشد من والطيور الصغيرة ينتظر في الخارج

all the little birds and animals rushed at Alice

هرعت كل الطيور الصغيرة إلى أليس

but she ran off as fast as she could

لكنها هربت بأسرع ما يمكن

and soon she found herself safe in a thick wood

وسرعان ما وجدت نفسها آمنة في خشب كثيف

Alice wandered about in the woods

تجولت أليس في الغابة

and she thought to herself:

وفكرت في نفسها:

"I know what I have to do first"

"أعرف ما يجب أن أفعله أولا"

"first I have to grow to my right size again"

"أولا يجب أن أنمو إلى حجمي الصحيح مرة أخرى"

"and then I have to find my way into that lovely garden"

"وبعد ذلك يجب أن أجد طريقي إلى تلك الحديقة الجميلة"

"I suppose I ought to eat or drink something or other"

"أفترض أنني يجب أن آكل أو أشرب شيئا أو آخر"

"but the question is what should I eat or drink?"

"لكن السؤال هو ماذا يجب أن آكل أو أشرب؟"

Alice looked all around her at the flowers

نظرت أليس من حولها إلى الزهور

and she looked through the blades of grass

ونظرت من خلال شفرات العشب

but she could not see anything to eat or drink

لكنها لم تستطع رؤية أي شيء تأكله أو تشربه

nothing looked like the right thing to eat or drink

لا شيء يبدو وكأنه الشيء الصحيح للأكل أو الشراب

There was a large mushroom growing near her

كان هناك فطر كبير ينمو بالقرب منها

the mushroom was about the same height as Alice

كان الفطر بنفس ارتفاع أليس تقريبا

She stretched herself up on tiptoes

مددت نفسها على رؤوس أصابعها

and she peeped over the edge of the mushroom

ونظرت إلى حافة الفطر

her eyes immediately met the eyes of a large blue caterpillar

التقت عيناها على الفور بعيون كاترببلر أزرق كبير

the caterpillar was sitting on the top of the mushroom

كانت اليرقة جالسة على قمة الفطر

and the caterpillar had crossed all his arms

وكانت اليرقة قد عبرت كل ذراعيه

and he was quietly smoking a long hookah

وكان يدخن بهدوء شيشة طويلة

and he took not the smallest notice of anything

ولم يأخذ أدنى اهتمام لأي شيء

and he certainly didn't pay attention to Alice

وهو بالتأكيد لم ينتبه إلى أليس

Advice from a caterpillar
نصيحة من كاترييلر

At last the caterpillar took the hookah out of its mouth

أخيرا أخرجت اليرقة الشيشة من فمها

and he addressed Alice in a languid, sleepy voice

وخاطب أليس بصوت ضعيف ونعاس

"Who are you?" said the caterpillar

"من أنت؟" قالت اليرقة

Alice replied, rather shyly, "I hardly know, sir"

أجابت أليس بخجل إلى حد ما ، "بالكاد أعرف يا سيدي"

"just at the moment it's all a bit..."

"فقط في الوقت الحالي ، كل شيء قليلا ..."

"I know who I was when I got up this morning""

"أعرف من كنت عندما استيقظت هذا الصباح"

"but I think I must have changed several times since then"

"لكنني أعتقد أنني يجب أن أكون قد تغيرت عدة مرات منذ ذلك الحين"

"What do you mean by that?" said the caterpillar

"ماذا تقصد بذلك؟" قالت اليرقة

sternly the caterpillar asked her to explain herself

طلبت منها اليرقة بصرامة أن تشرح نفسها

"I can't explain myself, I'm afraid, sir," said Alice

قالت أليس: "لا أستطيع أن أشرح ، أخشى يا سيدي"

"because I'm not myself"

"لأنني لست"

"you see, being so many different sizes in a day is very confusing"

"كما ترى ، فإن وجود أحجام مختلفة في يوم واحد أمر محير للغاية"

She pulled herself up and said very gravely:

سحبت نفسها وقالت بجدية شديدة:

"I think you ought to tell me who you are, first"

"أعتقد أنه يجب عليك أن تخبرني من أنت أولا"

"Why?" said the caterpillar

"لماذا؟" قالت اليرقة

Alice could not think of any good reason

لم تستطع أليس التفكير في أي سبب وجيه

and the caterpillar seemed to be in a very unpleasant state of mind

وبدا أن اليرقة في حالة ذهنية غير سارة للغاية

so she turned away

لذلك ابتعدت

"Come back!" the caterpillar called after her

"عد!" نادت اليرقة بعدها

"I've something important to say!"

"لدي شيء مهم لأقوله!"

Alice turned and came back again

استدارت أليس وعادت مرة أخرى

"Keep your temper," said the caterpillar

"حافظ على أعصابك" ، قالت اليرقة

"Is that all?" said Alice

"هل هذا كل شيء؟" قالت أليس

and she swallowed her anger as well as she could

وابتلعت غضبها قدر استطاعتها

"No," said the caterpillar

"لا" ، قالت اليرقة

the caterpillar unfolded its arms

كشفت اليرقة ذراعيها

and he took the hookah out of his mouth again

وأخرج الشيشة من فمه مرة أخرى

and he said, "So you think you're changed, do you?"

فقال ، "إذن تعتقد أنك قد تغيرت ، أليس كذلك؟"

"I'm afraid, I am changed, sir," said Alice

قالت أليس: "أخشى ، لقد تغيرت يا سيدي"

"I can't remember things as I used to remember them"

"لا أستطيع أن أتذكر الأشياء كما كنت أتذكرها"

"and I don't stay the same size for more than ten minutes!"

"وأنا لا أبقى بنفس الحجم لأكثر من عشر دقائق!"

"What size do you want to be?" asked the caterpillar

"ما هو الحجم الذي تريد أن تكون؟" سألت اليرقة

"Oh, I don't particularly mind what size I am," Alice hastily replied

"أوه ، لا أمانع بشكل خاص في حجمي" ، أجابت أليس على عجل

"I just don't like changing size so often, you know"

"أنا فقط لا أحب تغيير الحجم كثيرا ، كما تعلم"

"I would like to be a little larger, sir"

"أود أن أكون أكبر قليلا يا سيدي"

"if you wouldn't mind," added Alice

"إذا كنت لا تمانع" ، أضافت أليس

"Ten centimetres is such a wretched height to be"

"عشرة سنتيمترات هو ارتفاع بائس"

"It is a very good height indeed!" said the caterpillar angrily

"إنه ارتفاع جيد جدا حقا!" قالت اليرقة بغضب

and he reared itself upright as he spoke

ورفع نفسه منتصبا وهو يتحدث

he was exactly ten centimetres high

كان ارتفاعه عشرة سنتيمترات بالضبط

In a minute or two, the caterpillar got down off the mushroom

في دقيقة أو دقيقتين ، نزلت اليرقة من الفطر

and he crawled away into the grass

وزحف بعيدا في العشب

as he went away, he made some little remarks

وبينما كان يذهب بعيدا ، أدلى ببعض الملاحظات الصغيرة

"One side will make you grow taller"

"جانب واحد سيجعلك تنمو أطول"

"and the other side will make you grow shorter"

"والجانب الآخر سيجعلك تنمو أقصر"

"One side of what?" thought Alice to herself

"جانب واحد من ماذا؟" فكرت أليس في نفسها

"The other side of what?"

"الجانب الآخر من ماذا؟"

"the side of the mushroom," said the caterpillar

"جانب الفطر" ، قالت اليرقة

it was as if she had asked her question aloud

كان الأمر كما لو أنها سألت سؤالها بصوت عال

and in another moment, he was out of sight

وفي لحظة أخرى ، كان بعيدا عن الأنظار

Alice remained looking thoughtfully at the mushroom

ظلت أليس تنظر بعناية إلى الفطر

she was trying to make out which were the two sides of the mushroom

كانت تحاول معرفة جانبي الفطر

At last she stretched her arms around the mushroom

أخيرا مدت ذراعيها حول الفطر

and she broke off a bit of the edges

وقطعت قليلا من الحواف

"And now, which side is which?" she said to herself

"والآن ، أي جانب أيهما؟" قالت لنفسها

and she nibbled a little of the right-hand bit

وقضم القليل من اليد اليمنى

The next moment she felt a violent blow underneath her chin

في اللحظة التالية شعرت بضربة عنيفة تحت ذقنها

her chin had struck her foot!

أصابت ذقنها قدمها!

She was a good deal frightened by this very sudden change

كانت خائفة كثيرا من هذا التغيير المفاجئ للغاية

she was shrinking very rapidly

كانت تتقلص بسرعة كبيرة

so she quickly ate some of the other bit of mushroom

لذلك سرعان ما أكلت بعضا من الفطر الآخر

Her chin was pressed very closely against her foot

تم ضغط ذقنها عن كثب على قدمها

there was hardly room to open her mouth

بالكاد كان هناك مجال لفتح فمها

but she did at last manage to open her mouth

لكنها تمكنت أخيرا من فتح فمها

and she swallowed a morsel of the left-hand bit

وابتلعت لقمة من اليد اليسرى

"my head's been freed at last!" said Alice

"لقد تم تحرير رأسي أخيرا!" قالت أليس

she looked down at herself

نظرت إلى نفسها

but all she could see was an immense length of neck

لكن كل ما استطاعت رؤيته كان طولا هائلا للرقبة

her neck seemed to rise like a stalk

بدت رقبتها وكأنها ترتفع مثل ساق

and she looked down over a sea of green leaves

ونظرت إلى الأسفل فوق بحر من الأوراق الخضراء

"Where have my shoulders gotten to?"

"إلى أين وصلت كتفي؟"

"And oh, my poor hands, how is it I can't see you?"

"وأوه ، يدي المسكينة ، كيف لا أستطيع رؤيتك؟"

but her neck did have one benefit

لكن رقبتها كان لها فائدة واحدة

she could move her head in any direction

يمكنها تحريك رأسها في أي اتجاه

in fact, she was just like a serpent

في الواقع ، كانت مثل الثعبان

she gracefully zigzagged her head down

تعرجت رأسها برشاقة لأسفل

and she moved her head through the trees

وحركت رأسها عبر الأشجار

but then she heard a sharp hiss

لكنها سمعت بعد ذلك هسهسة حادة

and she quickly pulled her head back

وسرعان ما سحبت رأسها للخلف

a large pigeon had flown into her face

طار حمامة كبيرة في وجهها

and the pigeon was violently with its wings

وكان الحمام بعنف بجناحيه

"Serpent!" cried the pigeon

"الثعبان!" صرخ الحمام

"I'm not a serpent!" said Alice indignantly

"أنا لست ثعبانا!" قالت أليس بسخط

"Leave me alone!"

"اتركني وشأني!"

"I've tried the roots of trees"

"لقد جربت جذور الأشجار"

"and I've tried hedges," the pigeon went on

"وقد جربت التحوطات" ، تابع الحمام

"but those serpents! There's no pleasing them!"

"لكن تلك الثعابين! لا يوجد إرضاء لهم!"

Alice was more and more puzzled

كانت أليس في حيرة أكثر فأكثر

"As if it wasn't trouble enough hatching the eggs," said the pigeon

قال الحمامة: "كما لو لم تكن مشكلة كافية في تفقيس البيض"

"by night and day I must look out for serpents too!"

"ليلا ونهارا يجب أن أبحث عن الثعابين أيضا!"

"I had just found the highest tree in the forest"

"لقد وجدت للتو أعلى شجرة في الغابة"

"surely I'd be free from serpents here?"

"بالتأكيد سأكون حرا من الثعابين هنا؟"

"and out comes a serpent from the sky!"

"ويخرج ثعبان من السماء!"

"But I'm not a serpent, I tell you!" said Alice

"لكنني لست ثعبانا ، أقول لك!" قالت أليس

"I'm a... I'm a... I'm a little girl," she added rather doubtfully

"أنا ... أنا ... أنا فتاة صغيرة" ، أضافت بشك إلى حد ما

she had after all been going through a lot of changes

لقد مرت بعد كل شيء بالكثير من التغييرات

"You're looking for eggs," said the pigeon

قال الحمامة: "أنت تبحث عن البيض"

"I know that for a fact"

"أعرف ذلك على سبيل الحقيقة"

"and what does it matter if you're a little girl or a serpent?"

"وما الذي يهم إذا كنت فتاة صغيرة أو ثعبانا؟"

"It matters a good deal to me," said Alice hastily

"إنه يهمني كثيرا" ، قالت أليس على عجل

"but I'm not looking for eggs, as it happens"

"لكنني لا أبحث عن البيض ، كما يحدث"

"and I wouldn't want your eggs anyway"

"وأنا لا أريد بيضك على أي حال"

"I don't like my eggs raw"

"أنا لا أحب بيضتي نيئة"

"Well, be off then!" said the pigeon in a sulky tone

"حسنا ، ابتعد إذن!" قال الحمام بنبرة عاهبة

and the pigeon settled down again into its nest

واستقر الحمام مرة أخرى في عشه

Alice crouched down among the trees as well as she could

جثمت أليس بين الأشجار قدر استطاعتها

her neck kept getting entangled among the branches

ظلت رقبتها تتشابك بين الأغصان

every now and then she had to stop and untwist her neck

بين الحين والآخر كان عليها أن تتوقف وفك رقبتها

After awhile she remembered the mushroom

بعد فترة تذكرت الفطر

she still held the pieces of mushroom in her hands

كانت لا تزال تحمل قطع الفطر في يديها

and she set to work very carefully

وشرعت في العمل بعناية فائقة

first she nibbled at one piece

أولا قضمت قطعة واحدة

and then she nibbled at the other piece

ثم قضمت القطعة الأخرى

sometimes she grew taller

في بعض الأحيان كانت تنمو أطول

and sometimes she grew shorter

وأحيانا أصبحت أقصر

but finally she achieved her usual height

لكنها أخيرا حققت طولها المعتاد

she hadn't been her own height for some time

لم تكن طولها لبعض الوقت

so everything felt strange for a while

لذلك شعرت بغرابة كل شيء لفترة من الوقت

"The next thing to do is to get into that beautiful garden"

"الشيء التالي الذي يجب فعله هو الدخول إلى تلك الحديقة الجميلة"

"how is that to be done, I wonder?"

"كيف يتم ذلك ، أتساءل؟"

As she said this, she came upon an open place

عندما قالت هذا ، جاءت إلى مكان مفتوح
there was a little house, a bit higher than a metre
كان هناك منزل صغير ، أعلى قليلا من متر
"I wonder who lives in this little house"
"أتساءل من يعيش في هذا المنزل الصغير"
"I certainly can't go in as big as I am"
"بالتأكيد لا يمكنني الدخول بحجم أنا"
"I would frighten them terribly!"
"سأخيفهم بشكل رهيب!"
so she nibbled at the little mushroom again
لذلك قضمت الفطر الصغير مرة أخرى
and soon she brought herself down thirty centimetres
وسرعان ما انخفضت نفسها ثلاثين سنتيمترا

A pig and some pepper
خنزير وبعض الفلفل

For a minute or two she stood looking at the house

وقفت لمدة دقيقة أو دقيقتين تنظر إلى المنزل

suddenly a footman came running out of the woods

فجأة خرج رجل من الغابة

he was wearing a special livery uniform

كان يرتدي زيا خاصا

judging by his face only, she would have called him a fish

إذا حكمنا من خلال وجهه فقط ، كانت ستطلق عليه سمكة

and he rapped loudly at the door with his knuckles

وضرب بصوت عال عند الباب بمفاصل أصابعه

the door was opened by another footman

فتح الباب من قبل رجل آخر

this footman too was wearing a special livery

كان هذا الرجل يرتدي كسوة خاصة أيضا

this footman had a round face and large eyes like a frog

كان لهذا الرجل وجه مستدير وعينان كبيرتان مثل الضفدع

The footman that looked like a fish initiated the ceremony

بدأ الرجل الذي بدا وكأنه سمكة الحفل

he pulled out something from under his arm

أخرج شيئا من تحت ذراعه

and he pulled out from under his arm an envelope

وأخرج من تحت ذراعه مظروفا

and this envelope he handed over to the other footman

وهذا الظرف سلمه إلى المشاة الآخر

in a ceremonious tone he told him the orders

بنبرة احتفالية أخبره بالأوامر

"This message is for the Duchess"

"هذه الرسالة للدوقة"

"An invitation from the queen to play croquet"

"دعوة من الملكة للعب الكروكيه"

The footman that looked like a frog repeated the order

كرر الرجل الذي بدا وكأنه ضفدع الأمر

"from the queen"

"من الملكة"

"an invitation"

"دعوة"

"for the Duchess"

"من أجل الدوقة"

"playing croquet"

"لعب الكروكيه"

Then they both bowed low

ثم انحنى كلاهما

and the curls in their wigs got entangled together

وتشابكت الضفائر في الشعر المستعار معا

soon the footman that looked like a fish was gone

سرعان ما اختفى الرجل الذي بدا وكأنه سمكة

but the footman that looked like a frog was still there

لكن الرجل الذي بدا وكأنه ضفدع كان لا يزال هناك

he was sitting on the ground near the door

كان جالسا على الأرض بالقرب من الباب

he was staring stupidly up into the sky

كان يحدق بغباء في السماء

Alice went timidly up to the door and knocked

صعدت أليس بخجل إلى الباب وطرقت

"There's no use in knocking," said the footman

"لا فائدة من الطرق" ، قال الرجل

"and that is for two reasons"

"وذلك لسببين"

"First, because I'm on the same side of the door as you are"

"أولا ، لأنني على نفس الجانب من الباب مثلك"

"secondly, because they're making so much noise inside"

"ثانيا ، لأنهم يحدثون الكثير من الضوضاء في الداخل"

"no one could possibly hear you"

"لا أحد يمكن أن يسمعك"

And there certainly was a most extraordinary noise going on within

وبالتأكيد كان هناك ضجيج غير عادي يحدث في الداخل

a constant howling and sneezing

عواء وعطس مستمر

and every now and then a sound of great crashing

وبين الحين والآخر صوت تحطم كبير

as if a dish or kettle had been broken to pieces

كما لو أن طبقا أو غلاية قد تم تكسيرها إلى أشلاء

"How am I to get in?" asked Alice

"كيف يمكنني الدخول؟" سألت أليس

"Should you get in at all?" said the footman

"هل يجب أن تدخل على الإطلاق؟" قال الرجل

"That's the first question, you know"

"هذا هو السؤال الأول ، كما تعلم"

Alice opened the door and went in

فتحت أليس الباب ودخلت

The door led right into a large kitchen

أدى الباب مباشرة إلى مطبخ كبير

the kitchen was full of smoke from one end to the other

كان المطبخ مليئا بالدخان من طرف إلى آخر

in the middle of the kitchen was the Duchess

في منتصف المطبخ كانت الدوقة

she was sitting on a three-legged stool

كانت جالسة على كرسي ثلاثي الأرجل

and she was nursing a baby

وكانت ترضع طفلا

the cook was leaning over the fire

كان الطباخ يتكئ فوق النار

he was stirring a large caldron

كان يحرك ممثل كبير

and the caldron seemed to be full of soup

وبدا أن المكالدرون مليء بالحساء

"There's certainly too much pepper in that soup!" Alice said to herself

"بالتأكيد هناك الكثير من الفلفل في هذا الحساء!" قالت أليس لنفسها

she said it as best she could without sneezing

قالت ذلك بأفضل ما تستطيع دون أن تعطس

Even the Duchess sneezed occasionally

حتى الدوقة عطست من حين لآخر

but the baby's actions were the most noteworthy

لكن تصرفات الطفل كانت الأكثر جدارة بالملاحظة

the baby was sneezing and howling alternately

كان الطفل يعطس ويعوي بالتناوب

there was not a moment's pause between howling and sneezing

لم يكن هناك توقف للحظة بين العواء والعطس

There were two creatures in the kitchen that did not sneeze

كان هناك مخلوقان في المطبخ لم يعطسا

the cook was too busy to sneeze

كان الطباخ مشغولا جدا بحيث لا يستطيع العطس

and the large cat did not seem to mind the pepper

ولا يبدو أن القطة الكبيرة تمانع في الفلفل

instead, the large cat was grinning from ear to ear

بدلا من ذلك ، كانت القطة الكبيرة تبتسم من الأذن إلى الأذن

"Please would you tell me," said Alice, a little timidly

"من فضلك هل تخبرني" ، قالت أليس بخجل قليلا

"why is your cat grinning like that?"

"لماذا تبتسم قطتك هكذا؟"

"It's a Cheshire-Cat," said the Duchess

قالت الدوقة: "إنها قطة شيشاير"

"and that's why he's grinning from ear to ear"

"ولهذا السبب يبتسم من الأذن إلى الأذن"

"I didn't know that a Cheshire-Cat always grinned"

"لم أكن أعرف أن قطة شيشاير كانت دائما تبتسم"

"in fact, I didn't know that cats could grin," said Alice

قالت أليس: "في الواقع ، لم أكن أعرف أن القطط يمكن أن تبتسم"

"there is much you don't know," said the Duchess

قالت الدوقة: "هناك الكثير الذي لا تعرفه"

"there is much you don't know and that's a fact"

"هناك الكثير الذي لا تعرفه وهذه حقيقة"

Just then the cook took the caldron of soup off the fire

عندها فقط أزال الطباخ كالدرون الحساء من النار

and at once she started throwing everything within her reach

وعلى الفور بدأت في رمي كل شيء في متناول يدها

she threw everything she could at the Duchess and the babe

ألقت كل ما في وسعها على الدوقة والطفل

first she threw the fire-irons

أولا ألقت النار

then she threw a handful of saucepans

ثم ألقت حفنة من القدور

and finally she threw the plates and dishes

وأخيرا ألقت الأطباق والأطباق

The Duchess took no notice of her

لم تلاحظها الدوقة

even when she was hit by a plate she did not worry

حتى عندما أصيبت بلوحة لم تقلق

the baby was already howling so much

كان الطفل يعوي كثيرا بالفعل

so it was impossible to say whether the blows hurt the baby
or not

لذلك كان من المستحيل تحديد ما إذا كانت الضربات تؤذي الطفل أم لا

"Oh, please mind what you're doing!" cried Alice

"أوه ، من فضلك اهتم بما تفعله!" صرخت أليس

and she jumped up and down in an agony of terror

وقفزت صعودا وهبوطا في عذاب من الرعب

the Duchess offered Alice the baby

عرضت الدوقة على أليس الطفل

"Here! You may nurse the baby a bit, if you like!"

"هنا! يمكنك إرضاع الطفل قليلا ، إذا أردت!"

and she flung the baby at her as she spoke

وألقت الطفل عليها وهي تتحدث

"I must go and get ready to play croquet with the queen"

"يجب أن أذهب وأستعد للعب الكروكيه مع الملكة"

and she hurried out of the room

وخرجت من الغرفة

Alice caught the baby with some difficulty

أمسكت أليس بالطفل ببعض الصعوبة

because it was a very odd-shaped little creature

لأنه كان مخلوقا صغيرا غريبا جدا

and the baby held out its arms and legs in all directions

ورفع الطفل ذراعيه وساقيه في جميع الاتجاهات

"I better take this child away with me," thought Alice

"من الأفضل أن آخذ هذا الطفل معي" ، فكرت أليس

"they're sure to kill this baby in a day or two"

"من المؤكد أنهم سيقتلون هذا الطفل في يوم أو يومين"

"Wouldn't it be murder to leave this baby behind?"

"ألن يكون من القتل ترك هذا الطفل وراءه؟"

She said the last words out loud

قالت الكلمات الأخيرة بصوت عال

and the little thing grunted in reply

وشخر الشيء الصغير ردا على ذلك

"you best not turn into a pig, my dear," said Alice

قالت أليس "من الأفضل ألا تتحول إلى خنزير يا عزيزتي"

"or else I'll have nothing more to do with you"

"وإلا فلن يكون لدي أي علاقة بك أخرى"

Alice was just beginning to think to herself:

كانت أليس قد بدأت للتو في التفكير في نفسها:

"Now, what am I to do with this creature, when I get it home?"

"الآن ، ماذا أفعل بهذا المخلوق ، عندما أعود إليه إلى المنزل؟"

but then the little creature grunted a little violently

ولكن بعد ذلك شخر المخلوق الصغير بعنف قليلا

and Alice looked down into its face in some alarm

ونظرت أليس إلى وجهها في بعض الذعر

This time there could be no mistake about it

هذه المرة لا يمكن أن يكون هناك خطأ في ذلك

it was neither more nor less than a pig

لم يكن أكثر ولا أقل من خنزير

so she set the little creature down

لذلك وضعت المخلوق الصغير

and the little creature trot away quietly into the wood

ويهرول المخلوق الصغير بهدوء في الغابة

Alice felt quite relieved to see the creature go

شعرت أليس بالارتياح الشديد لرؤية المخلوق يذهب

Alice was a little startled by seeing the Cheshire-Cat

شعرت أليس بالذهول قليلا برؤية Cheshire-Cat

it was sitting on a bough of a tree a few yards off

كانت جالسة على غصن شجرة على بعد أمتار قليلة

The cat only grinned when it saw her

ابتسمت القطة ابتسامة عريضة فقط عندما رأتها

"Cheshire-cat," began Alice, rather timidly

"قطة شيشاير" ، بدأت أليس بخجل إلى حد ما

"would you please tell me which way I ought to go from
here?"

"هل تخبرني من فضلك في أي اتجاه يجب أن أذهب من هنا؟"

"In that direction," the cat said

قالت القطة: "في هذا الاتجاه"

and it waved the right paw around

ولوح بالمخلب الأيمن حوله

"In that direction lives a maker of hats"

"في هذا الاتجاه يعيش صانع القبعات"

and then the cat waved its other paw

ثم لوحت القطة بمخلبها الآخر

"and in that direction lives a march hare"

"وفي هذا الاتجاه يعيش أرنب مسيرة"

"Visit either you like; they're both mad"

"قم بزيارة أيا كانت تريد. كلاهما مجنون"

"But I don't want to go among mad people," Alice remarked

"لكنني لا أريد أن أذهب بين المجانين" ، قالت أليس

"Oh, you can't help that," said the Cat

"أوه ، لا يمكنك المساعدة في ذلك" ، قالت القطة

"we're all mad here"

"نحن جميعا غاضبون هنا"

"are you playing croquet with the queen today?"

"هل تلعب الكروكيه مع الملكة اليوم؟"

"I would like to very much," said Alice

قالت أليس "أود ذلك كثيرا"

"but I haven't been invited yet"

"لكنني لم تتم دعوتي بعد"

"You'll see me there," said the Cat

قالت القطة: "ستراني هناك"

and from one moment to the next the cat vanished

ومن لحظة إلى أخرى اختفت القطة

soon Alice got in sight of the house of the march hare

سرعان ما ظهرت أليس على مرأى من منزل أرنب المسيرة

this was a very large house

كان هذا منزلا كبيرا جدا

so Alice did not want to go near the house

لذلك لم ترغب أليس في الاقتراب من المنزل

first she had to nibble some more of the left side bit of mushroom

في البداية كان عليها أن تقضم المزيد من الجزء الأيسر من الفطر

a mad tea-party
حفلة شاي مجنونة

In front of the house there was a tree

أمام المنزل كانت هناك شجرة

and under the tree there was a table

وتحت الشجرة كانت هناك طاولة

and the table was set with all sorts of cutlery

وتم إعداد الطاولة بجميع أنواع أدوات المائدة

the march hare and the hat maker were at the table

كان أرنب المسيرة وصانع القبعات على الطاولة

and together they were having tea

وكانوا يتناولون الشاي معا

a dormouse was sitting between them

كان الزغب يجلس بينهما

and the dormouse was fast asleep

وكان الزغب نائما سريعا

The table was of extraordinary size

كان الجدول بحجم غير عادي

but most of the table was unoccupied

لكن معظم الطاولة كانت غير مأهولة

they sat crowded together at one corner of the table

جلسوا مزدحمين معا في أحد أركان الطاولة

and yet they made excuses when they saw Alice

ومع ذلك فقد اختلقوا الأعذار عندما رأوا أليس

"No room! No room!" they cried out

"لا مكان! لا مكان!" صرخوا

"There's plenty of room!" said Alice indignantly

"هناك متسع كبير!" قالت أليس بسخط

at one end of the table there was a large arm-chair

في أحد طرفي الطاولة كان هناك كرسي كبير بذراعين

and Alice sat herself in the armchair

وجلست أليس على الكرسي بذراعين

the hat maker opened his eyes very wide

فتح صانع القبعات عينيه على مصراعيه

he couldn't believe what he was seeing

لم يستطع تصديق ما كان يراه

but his mind was curious about other things

لكن عقله كان فضوليا بشأن أشياء أخرى

"Why is a raven like a writing-desk?"

"لماذا الغراب مثل مكتب الكتابة؟"

Alice was open to the challenge

كانت أليس منفتحة على التحدي

"I'm glad they've begun asking riddles"

"أنا سعيد لأنهم بدأوا في طرح الألغاز"

"I believe I can guess that," she added aloud

وأضافت بصوت عال: "أعتقد أنني أستطيع تخمين ذلك"

The march hare grew curious about Alice

أصبح أرنب المسيرة فضوليا بشأن أليس

"Do you really think you can find the answer?"

"هل تعتقد حقا أنه يمكنك العثور على الإجابة؟"

"I think I can find the answer indeed," said Alice

قالت أليس: "أعتقد أنني أستطيع العثور على الإجابة بالفعل"

"Then you should say what you mean," the march hare went
on

"إذن يجب أن تقول ما تعنيه" ، استمر أرنب المسيرة

"I do say what I mean," Alice hastily replied

"أنا أقول ما أعنيه" ، أجابت أليس على عجل

"at the very least I mean what I say"

"على الأقل أعني ما أقوله"

"that's the same thing, you know"

"هذا نفس الشيء ، كما تعلم"

the dormouse also contributed to the conversation

ساهم الزغب أيضا في المحادثة

but the dormouse seemed to be talking in its sleep

لكن بدا أن الزغب يتحدث أثناء نومه

"I breathe when I sleep"

"أتنفس عندما أنام"

"I sleep when I breathe!"

"أنام عندما أتنفس!"

"you might as well say they are the same too"

"يمكنك أيضا القول إنهما متماثلان أيضا"

"It is the same thing with you," said the hat maker

"إنه نفس الشيء معك" ، قال صانع القبعات

and he poured a little tea on the dormouse's nose

وسكب القليل من الشاي على أنف الdormouse

The Dormouse shook its head impatiently

هز الزغب رأسه بفارغ الصبر

and again the dormouse spoke, without opening its eyes

ومرة أخرى تحدث الزغب ، دون أن يفتح عينيه

"Of course, of course it is the same"

"بالطبع ، بالطبع هو نفسه"

"that's just what I was going to say myself"

"هذا بالضبط ما كنت سأقوله"

The hat maker turned to Alice and asked another question

التفت صانع القبعات إلى أليس وطرح سؤالا آخر

"Have you guessed the riddle yet?"

"هل خمنت اللغز بعد؟"

"No, I give up," Alice conceded

"لا ، أنا أستسلم" ، اعترفت أليس

"What's the answer?" she wanted to know

"ما هو الجواب؟" أرادت أن تعرف

"I haven't the slightest idea," said the hat maker

قال صانع القبعة: "ليس لدي أدنى فكرة"

"Nor do I know," said the march hare

"ولا أعرف" ، قال أرنب المسيرة

Alice gave a weary sigh

تنهدت أليس بالتعب

"there are better uses of time than riddles without answers"

" هناك استخدامات أفضل للوقت من الألغاز بدون إجابات"

"have some more tea," the march hare said to Alice, very earnestly

"تناول المزيد من الشاي" ، قال أرنب المسيرة لأليس بجدية شديدة

Alice was quite offended by the offer

شعرت أليس بالإهانة من العرض

"I've had not had tea yet," Alice replied

أجابت أليس: "لم أتناول الشاي بعد"

"therefore I can't have any more tea"

"لذلك لا يمكنني تناول المزيد من الشاي"

"You mean you can't have less tea," said the hat maker

قال صانع القبعة: "أنت تقصد أنه لا يمكنك تناول كمية أقل من الشاي"

"it's very easy to take more than nothing"

"من السهل جدا أن تأخذ أكثر من لا شيء"

At this, Alice got up and walked off

عند هذا ، نهضت أليس وخرجت

The dormouse fell asleep instantly

نام الزغب على الفور

and neither of the others took the least notice of her going

ولم ينتبه أي من الآخرين بذهابها

though she looked back once or twice

على الرغم من أنها نظرت إلى الوراء مرة أو مرتين

they were trying to put the dormouse into the tea-pot

كانوا يحاولون وضع الزغب في إبريق الشاي

"At any rate, I'll never go there again!" said Alice

"على أي حال ، لن أذهب إلى هناك مرة أخرى!" قالت أليس

and she walked her way through the woods

وسارت في طريقها عبر الغابة

"that was the stupidest tea-party I've ever been to"

"كان هذا أغبى حفلة شاي زرتها على الإطلاق"

Just as she said this, she noticed something

تماما كما قالت هذا ، لاحظت شيئا ما

one of the trees had a door leading right into it

كان لإحدى الأشجار باب يؤدي إليها مباشرة

"That's very interesting!" she thought

"هذا مثير جدا للاهتمام!" فكرت

"I think I may as well go through the door"

"أعتقد أنني قد أذهب أيضا من الباب"

And through the door she went

وذهبت عبر الباب

Once more she found herself in the long hall

مرة أخرى وجدت نفسها في القاعة الطويلة

again she was close to the little glass table

مرة أخرى كانت قريبة من الطاولة الزجاجية الصغيرة

she took the little golden key

أخذت المفتاح الذهبي الصغير

and she unlocked the door that led into the garden

وفتحت الباب المؤدي إلى الحديقة

Then she set to work nibbling at the mushroom

ثم شرعت في العمل على قضم الفطر

she had kept a piece of the mushroom in her pocket

كانت قد احتفظت بقطعة من الفطر في جيبها

and finally she was about a metre tall

وأخيرا كان طولها حوالي متر

then she walked down the little corridor

ثم سارت في الممر الصغير

and then she finally found herself in the beautiful garden

ثم وجدت نفسها أخيرا في الحديقة الجميلة

and she was among the bright flower and the cool fountains

وكانت بين الزهرة الزاهية والنوافير الباردة

The queen's croquet ground
أرض الكروكيه للملكة

A large rose-tree stood near the entrance of the garden

وقفت شجرة ورد كبيرة بالقرب من مدخل الحديقة

the roses growing on the tree were white

كانت الورود التي تنمو على الشجرة بيضاء

but there were three gardeners painting the rose

ولكن كان هناك ثلاثة بستانيين يرسمون الوردة

they were busily painting the roses red

كانوا مشغولين بطلاء الورود باللون الأحمر

and Alice was watching them paint the roses red

وكانت أليس تشاهدهم يرسمون الورود باللون الأحمر

and suddenly their eyes chanced to fall upon Alice

وفجأة صادفت عيونهم أن تسقط على أليس

Alice spoke a little timidly

تحدثت أليس بخجل قليلا

"Would you tell me, please;"

"هل تخبرني من فضلك ؛"

"why are you all painting those roses?"

"لماذا ترسم تلك الورود؟"

five and seven said nothing, but looked at two

خمسة وسبعة لم يقولوا شيئا ، لكنهم نظروا إلى اثنين

two spoke, in a low voice

تحدث اثنان بصوت منخفض

"Why, the fact is, you see, madam"

"لماذا ، الحقيقة هي ، كما ترى ، سيدتي"

"this here ought to have been a red rose-tree"

"كان يجب أن تكون هذه هنا شجرة وردة حمراء"

"and we put a white rose-tree in by mistake"

"ووضعنا شجرة وردة بيضاء عن طريق الخطأ"

"as you would agree, the queen must not find out"

"كما توافق ، يجب على الملكة ألا تكتشف ذلك"

"else we would all have our heads cut off"

"وإلا لكنا جميعا نقطع رؤوسنا"

"So you see, madam, we're doing our best"

"لذا ترون ، سيدتي ، نحن نبذل قصارى جهدنا"
card five had been anxiously looking across the garden
كانت البطاقة الخامسة تنظر بقلق عبر الحديقة
At this moment card five called out, "The queen! The
queen!"
في هذه اللحظة صرخت البطاقة الخامسة ، "الملكة! الملكة!"
and the three gardeners instantly scurried away
واندفع البستانيون الثلاثة على الفور بعيدا
and they threw themselves flat upon their faces
وألقوا بأنفسهم على وجوههم
There was a sound of many footsteps
كان هناك صوت خطى كثيرة
Alice looked around, eager to see the queen
نظرت أليس حولها ، حريصة على رؤية الملكة
At the start of the procession were ten soldiers
في بداية الموكب كان هناك عشرة جنود
their hands and feet were in the corners
كانت أيديهم وأقدامهم في الزوايا
and in their hands and feet were clubs
وفي أيديهم وأقدامهم الهراوات
next came the ten courtiers
بعد ذلك جاء رجال الحاشية العشرة
the courtiers were ornamented all over with diamonds
كان رجال الحاشية مزينين بالماس
After the courtiers came the royal children
بعد رجال الحاشية جاء الأطفال الملكيون
there were ten of the royal children
كان هناك عشرة من الأطفال الملكيين
and all the royal children were ornamented with hearts
وجميع الأبناء الملكيين مزينون بقلوب
Next came the guests; mostly kings and queens
بعد ذلك جاء الضيوف. معظمهم من الملوك والملكات
and among the kings and queen Alice saw someone
ومن بين الملوك والملكة رأت أليس شخصا ما
she saw again the white rabbit she had chased
رأت مرة أخرى الأرنب الأبيض الذي طاردته

The procession was followed the knave of hearts

تبع الموكب بسكين القلوب

he was carrying the king's crown

كان يحمل تاج الملك

and the king's crown was on a crimson velvet cushion

وكان تاج الملك على وسادة مخملية قرمزية

and then came the end of this grand procession

ثم جاءت نهاية هذا الموكب الكبير

and there at the end were the king and queen of hearts

وهناك في النهاية كان ملك وملكة القلوب

the procession came opposite to Alice

جاء الموكب مقابل أليس

and they all stopped and looked at her

وتوقفوا جميعا ونظروا إليها

and the queen said severely, "Who is this?"

فقالت الملكة بشدة ، "من هذا؟"

She said it to the Knave of Hearts

قالت ذلك لـKnave of Hearts

but he just bowed and smiled in reply

لكنه انحنى وابتسم ردا على ذلك

Alice spoke very politely

تحدثت أليس بأدب شديد

"My name is Alice, so please your majesty"

"اسمي أليس ، لذا أرجو جلالتك"

but she had other thoughts to herself

لكن كانت لديها أفكار أخرى لنفسها

"they're only a pack of cards, after all!"

"إنها مجرد حزمة من البطاقات ، بعد كل شيء!"

"Can you play croquet?" shouted the queen

"هل يمكنك لعب الكروكيه؟" صرخت الملكة

The question was evidently meant for Alice

من الواضح أن السؤال كان مخصصا لأليس

"Yes!" said Alice loudly

"نعم!" قالت أليس بصوت عال

"Come play then!" roared the queen

"تعال والعب إذن!" زأرت الملكة

a timid voice spoke to Alice

تحدث صوت خجول إلى أليس

"it's a very fine day!"

"إنه يوم جيد جدا!"

She was walking by the white rabbit

كانت تمشي بجانب الأرنب الأبيض

and the White Rabbit was peeping anxiously into her face

وكان الأرنب الأبيض يختلس النظر بقلق في وجهها

"a very fine day indeed," confirmed Alice

"يوم جيد جدا حقا" ، أكدت أليس

"Where's the duchess?"

"أين الدوقة؟"

"Hush! Hush!" said the Rabbit

"صمت! صمت!" قال الأرنب

"She's under sentence of execution"

"إنها محكوم عليها بالإعدام"

"What is she being executed for?" asked Alice

"لماذا يتم إعدامها؟" سألت أليس

"She scuffed the queen's ears," the rabbit began

"لقد جرجرت أذني الملكة" ، بدأ الأرنب

the queen shouted in a voice of thunder

صرخت الملكة بصوت الرعد

"Get to your places!"

"اذهب إلى أماكنك!"

and people began running about in all directions

وبدأ الناس يركضون في كل الاتجاهات

and they all tumbled up against each other

وسقطوا جميعا ضد بعضهم البعض

However, they got settled down in a minute or two

ومع ذلك ، استقروا في دقيقة أو دقيقتين

and then the game began

ثم بدأت اللعبة

Alice had never seen such a curious croquet ground

لم تر أليس مثل هذه الأرض الغريبة من قبل

the grass was all ridges and furrows

كان العشب كلها تلال وأخاديد

The croquet balls were real hedgehogs

كانت كرات الكروكيه قنافذ حقيقية

and the mallets were real flamingos

وكانت المطارق طيور النحام الحقيقية

and the soldiers stood on their hands and feet

ووقف الجنود على أيديهم وأقدامهم

because the arches was made from their bodies

لأن الأقواس كانت مصنوعة من أجسادهم

The players all played at once

لعب جميع اللاعبين في وقت واحد

nobody waited for their turns

لم ينتظر أحد أدوارهم

and everyone quarrelled with everyone

وتشاجر الجميع مع الجميع

and all were fighting for the hedgehogs

وكانوا جميعا يقاتلون من أجل القنافذ

soon the queen was in a furious passion

سرعان ما كانت الملكة في شغف غاضب

and she started stamping about and shouting

وبدأت تختم وتصرخ

"Chop off his head!"

"!اقطع رأسه"

"Chop off her head!"

"!اقطع رأسها"

"Chop all their heads off!"

"!اقطع كل رؤوسهم"

Again Alice thought to herself

مرة أخرى فكرت أليس في نفسها

"They're dreadfully fond of beheading people here"

"إنهم مغرمون بشكل رهيب بقطع رؤوس الناس هنا"

"the great wonder is that there's anyone left alive!"

"!العجب الكبير هو أن هناك أي شخص بقي على قيد الحياة"

She was looking about for some way of escape

كانت تبحث عن طريقة للهروب

she noticed a curious appearance in the air

لاحظت مظهرا غريبا في الهواء

"It's the Cheshire-cat," she said to herself

قالت لنفسها: "إنها قطة شيشاير"

"now I shall have somebody to talk to"

"الآن سيكون لدي شخص أتحدث إليه"

"How are you getting on?" said the cat

"كيف حالك؟" قالت القطة

"I don't think they play at all fairly," Alice said

قالت أليس: "لا أعتقد أنهم يلعبون بشكل عادل على الإطلاق"

and she had a rather complaining tone

وكان لديها نبرة شكوى إلى حد ما

"they all quarrel so dreadfully"

"كلهم يتشاجرون بشكل مخيف"

"one can't hear oneself speak"

"لا يمكن للمرء أن يسمع نفسه يتكلم"

"and they don't seem to play by any rules"

"ولا يبدو أنهم يلعبون بأي قواعد"

the cat asked Alice a question in a low voice

سألت القطة أليس سؤالا بصوت منخفض

"How do you like the queen?"

"كيف تحب الملكة؟"

"I don't like her at all," said Alice

قالت أليس: "أنا لا أحبها على الإطلاق"

Alice thought she might as well go back

اعتقدت أليس أنها قد تعود أيضا

she wanted to see how the game was going

أرادت أن ترى كيف تسير اللعبة

she went off in search of her hedgehog

ذهبت بحثا عن قنفذها

The hedgehog was busy fighting another hedgehog

كان القنفذ مشغولا بمحاربة قنفذ آخر

this was an excellent opportunity

كانت هذه فرصة ممتازة

she could croquet one hedgehog with the other

يمكنها كروكيه قنفذ واحد مع الآخر

but her flamingo was on the other side of the garden

لكن طيور النحام كانت على الجانب الآخر من الحديقة

the flamingo was rather clumsy

كان طيور النحام أخرق إلى حد ما

her flamingo was trying to fly up into a tree

كانت فلامنغو تحاول الطيران إلى شجرة

She caught the flamingo by the leg

أمسكت بطائر النحام من ساقها

and she tucked the flamingo away under her arm

ووضعت طيور النحام بعيدا تحت ذراعها

that way the flamingo couldn't escape again

بهذه الطريقة لم يستطع فلامنغو الهروب مرة أخرى

Just then Alice happened to meet the duchess

عندها فقط التقت أليس بالدوقة

The duchess was now out of prison

كانت الدوقة الآن خارج السجن

She tucked her arm affectionately under Alice's arm

وضعت ذراعها بمودة تحت ذراع أليس

and then they walked off together

ثم انطلقوا معا

Alice was very glad to find her in such a pleasant temper

كانت أليس سعيدة جدا بالعثور عليها في مثل هذا المزاج اللطيف

She was a little startled, however

ومع ذلك ، كانت مندهشة بعض الشيء

she heard the voice of the duchess close to her ear

سمعت صوت الدوقة بالقرب من أذنها

"You're thinking about something, my dear"

"أنت تفكر في شيء ما يا عزيزي"

"and that makes you forget to talk"

"وهذا يجعلك تنسى التحدث"

"The game's going on rather better now," Alice said

قالت أليس: "اللعبة تسير بشكل أفضل الآن"

it was one way of keeping the conversation going

كانت إحدى الطرق للحفاظ على استمرار المحادثة

"it is so indeed," said the duchess

قالت الدوقة: "إنه كذلك بالفعل"

"and the moral of that is this:"

"والمغزى من ذلك هو:"

"It is love that does it all!"

"الحب هو الذي يفعل كل شيء!"

"Love is what makes the world go around"

"الحب هو ما يجعل العالم يدور"

Alice had another explanation

كان لدى أليس تفسير آخر

"it's done by everybody minding his own business!"

"يتم ذلك من قبل الجميع الذين يهتمون بشؤونه الخاصة!"

"Ah, well! You could be right"

"آه ، حسنا! يمكن أن تكون على حق"

"It all means much the same thing," said the Duchess

قالت الدوقة: "كل هذا يعني نفس الشيء إلى حد كبير"

and she dug her sharp little chin into Alice's shoulder

وحفرت ذقنها الصغيرة الحادة في كتف أليس

"and the moral of that is this"

"والمغزى من ذلك هو هذا"

"Take care of the sense"

"اعتني بالإحساس"

"and then the sounds will take care of themselves"

"وبعد ذلك ستعتني الأصوات بنفسها"

but then the duchess's arm began to tremble

ولكن بعد ذلك بدأت ذراع الدوقة ترتجف

Alice looked up and there stood the queen

نظرت أليس إلى الأعلى ووقفت الملكة

the queen had her arms folded

كانت الملكة مطوية ذراعيها

and she was frowning like a thunderstorm!

وكانت عبوسة مثل عاصفة رعدية!

"I give you fair warning," shouted the queen

"أعطيك تحذيرا عادلا" ، صرخت الملكة

and she stomped on the ground as she spoke

وداست على الأرض وهي تتحدث

"either your head or her head must be off"

"إما أن يكون رأسك أو رأسها قبالة"

"Take your choice!"

"خذ اختيارك!"

"and be quick about it"

"وكن سريعا في ذلك"

The duchess made her choice

اتخذت الدوقة اختيارها

and within a moment the duchess was gone

وفي غضون لحظة ذهبت الدوقة

Then the queen spoke to Alice

ثم تحدثت الملكة إلى أليس

"Let's go on with the game"

"دعنا نواصل اللعبة"

Alice was too frightened to say a word

كانت أليس خائفة جدا من أن تقول كلمة واحدة

and she slowly followed her back to the croquet-ground

وتبعتها ببطء إلى أرض الكروكيه

the whole time the queen quarrelled with the other players

طوال الوقت تشاجرت الملكة مع اللاعبين الآخرين

"Chop off his head!"

"اقطع رأسه!"

"Chop off her head!"

"اقطع رأسها!"

"Chop all their heads off!"

"اقطع كل رؤوسهم!"

soon all the players were in custody

سرعان ما تم احتجاز جميع اللاعبين

only the king, the queen, and Alice remained

بقي فقط الملك والملكة وأليس

Then the queen left, quite out of breath

ثم غادرت الملكة ، وهي تتنفس تماما

and she walked away with Alice

وابتعدت مع أليس

Alice heard the king quietly say something

سمعت أليس الملك يقول شيئا بهدوء

"You are all pardoned"

"لقد عفوا عنكم جميعا"

but suddenly there was another cry heard

لكن فجأة سمعت صرخة أخرى

"The trial is beginning!"

"المحاكمة تبدأ!"

and Alice ran along with the others

وركضت أليس مع الآخرين

who stole the tarts?
من سرق الفطائر؟

The king and queen of hearts were seated

جلس ملك وملكة القلوب

they were on their throne when Alice arrived

كانوا على عرشهم عندما وصلت أليس

there was a great crowd assembled around them

كان هناك حشد كبير متجمعا حولهم

there were all sorts of little birds and beasts

كان هناك كل أنواع الطيور والوحوش الصغيرة

and there was the whole pack of cards

وكانت هناك حزمة كاملة من البطاقات

the knave was standing in front of them, in chains

كان المقبض يقف أمامهم ، مقيدا بالسلاسل

and there was a soldier on each side to guard him

وكان هناك جندي على كل جانب لحراسته

near the King was the white rabbit

بالقرب من الملك كان الأرنب الأبيض

he had a trumpet in one hand

كان لديه بوق في يد واحدة

and he had a scroll of parchment in the other hand

وكان لديه لفافة من المخطوطات في اليد الأخرى

In the very middle of the court was a table

في منتصف المحكمة كانت هناك طاولة

on the table was a large dish of tarts

على الطاولة كان هناك طبق كبير من الفطائر

"I wish they'd get the trial done," Alice thought

"أتمنى أن ينجزوا المحاكمة" ، فكرت أليس

"then we could eat some of those refreshments!"

"ثم يمكننا أن نأكل بعض تلك المرطبات!"

The judge, by the way, was the king

بالمناسبة ، كان القاضي هو الملك

and he wore his crown over his great wig

وارتدى تاجه فوق شعر مستعار كبير

"That's the jury-box," thought Alice

"هذا هو صندوق هيئة المحلفين" ، فكرت أليس

"and those twelve creatures, I suppose they are the jurors"

"وتلك المخلوقات الاثني عشر ، أفترض أنها المحلفون"

some were animals, and some were birds

كان بعضها وبعضها طيورا

Just then the white rabbit cried out

عندها فقط صرخ الأرنب الأبيض

"Silence in the court!"

"الصمت في المحكمة!"

"Herald, read the accusation!" said the king

"هيرالد ، اقرأ الاتهام!" قال الملك

the white rabbit blew three blasts on the trumpet

فجر الأرنب الأبيض ثلاث انفجارات على البوق

then he unrolled the parchment-scroll

ثم قام بفتح لفيفة المخطوطة

and he read as follows:

وقرأ على النحو التالي:

"The queen of hearts, she made some tarts,"

"ملكة القلوب ، صنعت بعض الفطائر ،"

"All this she did on a summer day"

"كل هذا فعلته في يوم صيفي"

"The knave of hearts, he stole those tarts"

"سكين القلوب ، سرق تلك الفطائر"

"And he took those tarts far away!"

"وأخذ تلك الفطائر بعيدا!"

"Call the first witness," said the king

قال الملك: "استدع الشاهد الأول"

and the white rabbit blew three blasts on the trumpet

وفجر الأرنب الأبيض ثلاث انفجارات على البوق

"bring the first witness!" he called out

"أحضر الشاهد الأول!" صرخ

The first witness was the hat maker

كان الشاهد الأول صانع القبعات

he came in with a teacup in one hand

جاء بفنجان شاي في يد واحدة

and he had a piece of bread and butter in the other hand

وكان لديه قطعة خبز وزبدة في اليد الأخرى

"You ought to have finished," said the King

قال الملك: "كان يجب أن تكون قد انتهيت"

"When did you begin?"

"متى بدأت؟"

The hat maker looked at the march hare

نظر صانع القبعات إلى أرنب المسيرة

the march hare had followed him into the court

تبعه أرنب المسيرة إلى المحكمة

he had walked arm in arm with the dormouse

كان يمشي جنبا إلى جنب مع الزغب

"Fourteenth of March, I think it was," he said

قال: "الرابع عشر من مارس ، أعتقد أنه كان"

"Give your evidence," said the king

قال الملك: "قدم شهادتك"

"and don't be nervous, or I'll have you executed on the spot"

"ولا تكن متوترا ، وإلا سأعدمك على الفور"

This did not seem to encourage the witness at all

لا يبدو أن هذا يشجع الشاهد على الإطلاق

he kept shifting from one foot to the other

استمر في التحول من قدم إلى أخرى

and he looked uneasily at the queen

ونظر بقلق إلى الملكة

and, in his confusion, he bit a large piece out of his teacup

وفي ارتباكه ، عض قطعة كبيرة من فنجان الشاي الخاص به

really he meant to bite from his bread and butter

حقا كان يقصد أن يعض من خبزه وزبدته

Just at this moment Alice felt a very curious sensation

في هذه اللحظة فقط شعرت أليس بإحساس فضولي للغاية

she was beginning to grow larger again

كانت قد بدأت تتنمو بشكل أكبر مرة أخرى

The miserable hat maker dropped his teacup

أسقط صانع القبعات البائس فنجان الشاي الخاص به

and the bread and butter fell to the ground

وسقط الخبز والزبدة على الأرض

and he went down on one knee

ونزل على ركبة واحدة

"I'm a poor man, your majesty," he began

"أنا رجل فقير ، جلالة الملك" ، بدأ

"You're a very poor speaker," said the king

قال الملك: "أنت متحدث فقير جدا"

"You may go," said the king

قال الملك: "يمكنك الذهاب"

and the hat maker hurriedly left the court

وغادر صانع القبعات الملعب على عجل

"Call the next witness!" said the king

"استدع الشاهد التالي!" قال الملك

The next witness was the duchess's cook

كان الشاهد التالي طباخ الدوقة

She carried the pepper-box in her hand

حملت صندوق الفلفل في يدها

and the people near the door began sneezing all at once

وبدأ الناس بالقرب من الباب في العطس دفعة واحدة

"Give your evidence," said the king

قال الملك: "قدم شهادتك"

"I shall give no evidence," said the cook

قال الطباخ: "لن أقدم أي دليل"

The king looked anxiously at the white rabbit

نظر الملك بقلق إلى الأرنب الأبيض

and the white rabbit spoke in a quiet voice

وتحدث الأرنب الأبيض بصوت هادئ

"your majesty must cross-examine this witness"

"يجب على جلالتك استجواب هذا الشاهد"

"Well, if I must, I must," the king said

قال الملك: "حسنا ، إذا كان لا بد لي ، يجب أن أفعل ذلك"

"What are tarts made of?"

"مما تصنع الفطائر؟"

"tarts are made of pepper, mostly," said the cook

قال الطباخ: "الفطائر مصنوعة من الفلفل في الغالب"

For some minutes the whole court was in confusion

لبضع دقائق كانت المحكمة بأكملها في حالة ارتباك

eventually they all settled down again

في النهاية استقروا جميعا مرة أخرى

but by then the cook had disappeared

ولكن بحلول ذلك الوقت كان الطباخ قد اختفى

"Never mind!" said the king

"لا تهتم!" قال الملك

"call to the stand the next witness"

"دعوة الشاهد التالي إلى المنصة"

Alice watched the white rabbit as he fumbled over the list

شاهدت أليس الأرنب الأبيض وهو يتعثر في القائمة

you can imagine her surprise at what she heard next

يمكنك أن تتخيل دهشتها مما سمعته بعد ذلك

at the top of his shrill little voice, he called the name "Alice!"

في الجزء العلوي من صوته الصغير الحاد ، أطلق على اسم "أليس!"

Alice's evidence
دليل أليس

"Here!" cried Alice

"هنا!" صرخت أليس

She jumped up in a great hurry

قفزت على عجل كبير

and she tipped over the jury-box

وانقلبت على صندوق هيئة المحلفين

and she knocked over all the jurymen

وأطاحت بجميع أعضاء هيئة المحلفين

and they fell on to the heads of the crowd below

وسقطوا على رؤوس الحشد أدناه

Alice was in great dismay

كانت أليس في حالة من الفزع الشديد

"Oh, I beg your pardon!" she exclaimed

"أوه ، أطلب العفو!" صرخت

"The trial cannot proceed," said the king

قال الملك: "لا يمكن أن تستمر المحاكمة"

"the jurymen must get back in their proper places"

"يجب على أعضاء هيئة المحلفين العودة إلى أماكنهم الصحيحة"

he repeated the order with great emphasis

كرر الأمر بتركيز كبير

and he looked at Alice sternly

ونظر إلى أليس بصرامة

"What do you know about these events?" the king asked Alice

"ماذا تعرف عن هذه الأحداث؟" سأل الملك أليس

"I know nothing on the subject," said Alice

قالت أليس: "لا أعرف شيئا عن هذا الموضوع"

The king then read from his book

ثم قرأ الملك من كتابه

"Rule forty two"

"القاعدة الثانية والأربعون"

"All persons more than a mile high are to leave the court"

"يجب على جميع الأشخاص الذين يزيد ارتفاعهم عن ميل واحد مغادرة

"I'm not a mile high," said Alice

قالت أليس: "أنا لست على ارتفاع ميل واحد"

"Nearly two miles high," said the Queen

قالت الملكة: "ما يقرب من ميلين"

"Well, I refuse to go," said Alice

قالت أليس: "حسنا ، أنا أرفض الذهاب"

The king turned pale

أصبح الملك شاحبا

and he shut his note-book hastily

وأغلق دفتر ملاحظاته على عجل

"Consider your verdict," he said to the jury

قال لهيئة المحلفين: "ضع في اعتبارك حكمك"

he spoke in a low, trembling voice

تحدث بصوت منخفض يرتجف

then the white rabbit spoke

ثم تحدث الأرنب الأبيض

"There's more evidence to come yet"

" هناك المزيد من الأدلة القادمة حتى الآن"

and he jumped up in a great hurry

وقفز على عجل كبير

"This paper has just been picked up"

"تم التقاط هذه الورقة للتو"

"It seems to be a letter written by the prisoner"

"يبدو أنها رسالة كتبها السجين"

He unfolded the paper as he spoke

فتح الورقة وهو يتحدث

"It isn't a letter, after all"

"إنها ليست رسالة ، بعد كل شيء"

"what it was was a set of verses"

"ما كان عليه مجموعة من الآيات"

"Please, your majesty," said the knave

"من فضلك ، جلالة الملك" ، قال السكين

"I didn't write those verses"

"لم أكتب تلك الآيات"

"and they can't prove that I wrote anything"

"ولا يمكنهم إثبات أنني كتبت أي شيء"

"there's no name signed at the end"

"لا يوجد اسم موقع في النهاية"

the king spoke to the knave

تحدث الملك إلى الكناف

"You must have meant to cause some mischief"

"لا بد أنك قصدت التسبب في بعض الأذى"

"else you'd have signed your name like an honest man"

"وإلا كنت ستوقع اسمك كرجل نزيه"

There was a general clapping of hands

كان هناك تصفيق عام للأيدي

and the king turned to the white rabbit

والتفت الملك إلى الأرنب الأبيض

"Read the verses," he ordered

"اقرأ الآيات" ، أمر

There was dead silence in the court

ساد صمت ميت في المحكمة

and the white rabbit read out the verses

وقرأ الأرنب الأبيض الآيات

They told me you had been to her

أخبروني أنك كنت معها

And they mentioned me to him

وذكروني له

She gave me a good character

لقد أعطتني شخصية جيدة

But she said I could not swim

لكنها قالت إنني لا أستطيع السباحة

He sent them word I had not gone

أرسل لهم كلمة لم أذهب

We know it to be true

نحن نعلم أن هذا صحيح

If she should push the matter on, what would become of you?

إذا كان عليها أن تدفع الأمر ، فماذا سيحدث لك؟

I gave her one, they gave him two

أعطيتها واحدة ، وأعطوه اثنين

You gave us three or more

لقد أعطيتنا ثلاثة أو أكثر

They all returned from him to you

لقد عادوا منه جميعا إليك

although they were mine before

على الرغم من أنهم كانوا لي من قبل

If I or she should chance to be

إذا كان يجب أن أكون أو هي فرصة

If I or she were involved in this affair

إذا كنت متورطا في هذه القضية

He trusts to you to set them free

إنه يثق بك لتحريرهم

Exactly as we were

تماما كما كنا

My notion was that you had been

كانت فكرتي أنك كنت

Before she had this fit

قبل أن يكون لديها هذا النوبة

An obstacle that came between

عقبة جاءت بين

Him, and ourselves, and it

هو ، وأنفسنا ، وهو

Don't let him know she liked them best

لا تدعه يعرف أنها أحبتهم أكثر

For this must for ever be a secret, kept from all the rest

لأن هذا يجب أن يكون سرا إلى الأبد ، مخفيا عن البقية

This secret must remain a secret between yourself and me

يجب أن يظل هذا السر سرا بيني وبينك

the king was very impressed

أعجب الملك كثيرا

"That's the most important piece of evidence we've heard
yet"

"هذا هو أهم دليل سمعناه حتى الآن"

"I don't believe those verses carry an atom of meaning,"
objected Alice

"لا أعتقد أن هذه الآيات تحمل ذرة من المعنى" ، اعترضت أليس

the King had his own opinion on the matter

كان للملك رأيه الخاص في هذه المسألة

"If there's no meaning in those words, that saves a world of
trouble"

"إذا لم يكن هناك معنى لهذه الكلمات ، فهذا ينقذ عالما من المتاعب"

"then we needn't try to find the meaning"

"إذن لا نحتاج إلى محاولة العثور على المعنى"

"Let the jury consider their verdict"

"دع هيئة المحلفين تنظر في حكمهم"

"No, no!" said the queen

"لا لا!" قالت الملكة

"Sentencing first—verdict afterwards"

"الحكم أولا ـ الحكم بعد ذلك"

"Stuff and nonsense!" said Alice loudly

"الاشياء والهراء!" قالت أليس بصوت عال

"how silly it is to sentence the defendant first!"

"كم هو سخيف أن نحكم على المدعى عليه أولا!"

"Hold your tongue!" said the queen, turning purple

"امسك لسانك!" قالت الملكة ، وتحولت إلى اللون الأرجواني

"I will not hold my tongue!" said Alice

"لن أمسك لساني

the queen shouted at the top of her voice

صرخت الملكة بأعلى صوتها

"chop off her head!"

"اقطع رأسها!"

Nobody made a movement

لم يقم أحد بحركة

"Who cares what you say?" said Alice

"من يهتم بما تقول؟" قالت أليس

she had grown to her full size by this time

كانت قد نمت إلى حجمها الكامل بحلول هذا الوقت

"You're nothing but a pack of cards!"

"أنت لست سوى حزمة من البطاقات!"

At this, all the cards rose up in the air

في هذا ، ارتفعت جميع البطاقات في الهواء

and all the cards came flying down upon her

وسقطت عليها كل البطاقات

she gave a little scream

أعطت القليل من الصراخ

she was half afraid, but also angry

كانت نصف خائفة ، لكنها غاضبة أيضا

and she tried to fight the cards off of herself

وحاولت محاربة الأوراق من نفسها

and then she found herself lying on the grass bank

ثم وجدت نفسها مستلقية على الضفة العشبية

her head was in the lap of her sister

كان رأسها في حضن أختها

some dead leaves had landed on her face

سقطت بعض الأوراق الميتة على وجهها

and her sister was gently brushing the leaves away

وكانت أختها تنظف الأوراق برفق

"Wake up, Alice dear!" said her sister

"استيقظي يا أليس العزيزة!" قالت أختها

"what a long sleep you've had!"

"يا له من نوم طويل قضيته!"

"Oh, I've had such a curious dream!" said Alice

"أوه ، لقد كان لدي مثل هذا الحلم الغريب!" قالت أليس

And she told her sister all she could remember

وأخبرت أختها بكل ما يمكن أن تتذكره

all the strange adventures that you have just been reading about

كل المغامرات الغريبة التي كنت تقرأ عنها للتو

Alice got up and ran off

نهضت أليس وركضت

and she thought, while she ran, about her dream

وفكرت ، بينما كانت تركض ، في حلمها

"what a wonderful dream it had been!"

"يا له من حلم رائع كان!"

www.ingramcontent.com/pod-product-compliance
Lightning Source LLC
Chambersburg PA
CBHW011051190726
48290CB00011B/3097